CARAMELLE & CARMILLA

CARAMELLE & CARMILLA

JEWELLE GOMEZ   J. SHERIDAN LE FANU

Aunt Lute

San Francisco

Aunt Lute Books, P.O. Box 410687, San Francisco, CA 94141

www.auntlute.com

Cover design: Helen Shewolf Tseng

Text design: Sarah Lopez

Editorial: Shay Brawn and Emma Rosenbaum

Production Team: María Mínguez Arias, Isis Asare, Golda Sargento, Erin Edge

An earlier version of "Caramelle" was published in "From Where We Sit" Tiny Satchel Press 2011.

The production of this book was made possible by support from California Arts Council, the Council on Literary Magazines and Publishers, the Poetry Foundation, the San Francisco Arts Commission, Sara and Two C-Dogs Foundation, and the Zellerbach Foundation.

Print ISBN: 978-1-951874-09-4

eBook ISBN: 978-1-939904-45-4

10 9 8 7 6 5 4 3 2 1

TABLE OF CONTENTS

THE POWER OF THE HAND: *CARMILLA AND CARAMELLE*

BY JEWELLE GOMEZ

"One sign of the vampire is the power of the hand."[1] So declares Joseph Sheridan Le Fanu at the end of his classic novella, *Carmilla*, originally published in the United Kingdom in 1872; predating Stoker's *Dracula* by twenty-five years. To contemporary readers this signifier identified by Le Fanu is ironic in light of the erotic lesbian nature of his story. It has deeper significance for me when I consider *Carmilla* as a precursor and partial inspiration of my own lesbian vampire novel, *The Gilda Stories* (1991).[2]

My short story, *Caramelle (2011)*, paired here with the Le Fanu novella is a part of the Gildaverse (as the young people might say) and amplifies the idea raised in Le Fanu's novella: much power resides in women and lesbians. Le Fanu's story is an early example of the principle that writing in speculative genres (horror, ghostly, science fiction, etc.) affords the author a better opportunity to represent situations and characters not usually acceptable in "literary" fiction.

---

1. Joseph Sheridan Le Fanu, *Carmilla* (London: Arcturus Publishing Limited 2023) 127.

2. Jewelle Gomez, *The Gilda Stories*, current publisher San Francisco, CA: City Lights Publishing 2016.

Joseph Thomas Sheridan Le Fanu (1814-1873) was born in Ireland, like many of the most famous writers who followed him, such as Bram Stoker (1847-1912), Robert Louis Stevenson (1850-1894) and Oscar Wilde (1854-1900). Immensely popular and very prolific, he published short stories, novels, and novellas, and was called "absolutely in the first rank as a writer of ghost stories."[3] Much of his writing was in the Gothic or Romantic genre so popular in the Victorian period, a genre often characterized by a pervasive mood of unnamed fears, trepidation, and a haunting sensibility, all amplified by dark, tempestuous weather, gloomy mansions, shadowy, wooded surroundings, unnamed, howling animals, and menacing servants.

The Victorian Era (1837-1901) in Great Britain was characterized by conflicting elements: dogmatic Christian religious practices alongside Christian mysticism. The spiritualist movement including mesmerism, mind-reading, and most popularly clairvoyance possibly, I imagine, emerged from the horrors of the extensive casualties of the Napoleonic Wars (1799-1815) which contributed to an impulse in the population to reach out to loved ones on "the other side."

This spirituality ironically developed alongside the increasing influence of science and technology over everyday life. People's lives began to be reshaped by increased industrialization, a shift

---

3. Julia Briggs, J.M. Rhodes, quoted in Jack Sullivan's *The Penguin Encyclopedia of Horror and the Supernatural*, (New York: Viking 1986) 233.

from farming to manufacturing, broadening availability of train travel, and improved modes of lighting, plumbing, and heating.[4]

These two contrasting aspects of modern life in industrializing England—spiritualism and scientific improvements—engendered gothic impulses in a proliferation of popular writers such as Charlotte Bronte (*Jane Eyre*), Robert Louis Stevenson (*Strange Case of Dr Jekyll and Mr Hyde*) Oscar Wilde (*The Picture of Dorian Gray*), and Mary Shelley (*Frankenstein*). Charles Dickens, whose work most often emerged from an economic social conscience tinged with sentimentalism, even used ghostly devices to deliver his message in works such as *A Christmas Carol* and the subsequent parts of his Christmas trilogy *Cricket on the Hearth* and *The Chimes: A Goblin Story*.

For a plethora of reasons (which are examined in larger histories),[5] one of the preeminent preoccupations during the Victorian Era's increasing wealth and expansion of empire was the control of female power. Economic control, certainly a most obvious objective, was often enforced through circumscription of female social life; for example: arranged marriages, male primogeniture, precariousness of female moral reputation, ease of committing independent-thinking women to asylums, and the suppression of sexual desire in cultured women. Popular 19th century literature,

4. Kristine Hughes, *The Writer's Guide to Everyday Life in Regency and Victorian England* (Cincinnati, Ohio: Writers Digest Books 1998) pp 6-15.

5. Sharon Marcus, *Between Women: Friendship, Desire, and Marriage in Victorian England* (Princeton, New Jersey: Princeton University Press) 2007; Ben Griffin, *The Politics of Gender in Victorian Britain* (Cambridge, UK: Cambridge University Press) 2012.

from the many novels of Mrs. Gaskill (1810-1865) and the perennially admired George Eliot (1819-1880; aka Mary Ann Evans) give contemporary readers the opportunity to see exactly how Victorian England and other societies used these tactics to control women and money.

With Carmilla Le Fanu departed somewhat from the traditional depiction of the inert and decorative female ideal in upper class society by introducing not only the vampire element which shaped Carmilla's "unseemly" desires and determination to win her goals but also Laura's eager curiosity. It was considered sinful and socially unacceptable for women to harbor sexual desires, or worse, to discuss or act on them, which makes Le Fanu's characterization of Carmilla's feelings surprising and possibly shocking to his contemporaries. With a rare insight, Le Fanu is able to portray those feelings as both pastoral and fearsome. However, Le Fanu's ultimate adherence to the values held dear by society pre-determined a tragic end to the story, reassuring Victorian readers that women with such desires could come to no good end.

Le Fanu frames the story as a "casebook of Dr Hesselius," an investigator of reports on the occult. This familiar method gives the story some legitimacy so readers feel less like voyeurs. The writer then offers a complex contrast of place, circumstance, and characters throughout the story. Before Laura even meets Carmilla she has been trained by her governesses to a two-sided perception of her life making her "a little shy, as lonely people are,"[6] while at

---

6. Le Fanu, *Carmilla*, 76.

the same time she experiences curiosity as "a restless and unscrupulous passion..."[7]

While Gothic fiction is most frequently considered "dark," that is shadowy, cloudy, grim castles, etc., Le Fanu's description of Laura's castle as she looks out over its surroundings is repeatedly the opposite: "no softer, sweeter scene could be imagined."[8] This frequent softening of the surroundings gives the sensuality that infuses the encounters between Laura and Carmilla a kinder, less stark context.

When I first read *Carmilla* in the 1980s I was disappointed in the depiction of female desire as predatory and murderous. As I was researching my own lesbian vampire story I wished for more optimistic inspiration. But on further study I understood Le Fanu had little opportunity to write that inspiration even if he could step out of his own Victorian upbringing. He was unable to separate lesbian desire from "the lusts and malignity of hell."[9] Nor could he imagine depicting female and lesbian sexuality as natural and healthy any more than he could avoid making his one reference to a Black character negative, referring to "a hideous black woman... nodding and grinning derisively..."[10] This is a not unexpected gibe given the historical context.

What Le Fanu does provide is multiple examples of the language of desire between women. Laura immediately observes Carmilla's many enticing qualities, including her hair: "so magnificently

7. Le Fanu, *Carmilla*, 81.
8. Le Fanu, *Carmilla*, 63.
9. Le Fanu, *Carmilla*, 128.
10. Le Fanu, *Carmilla*, 72.

thick and long when it was down about her shoulders; I have often placed my hands under it..."[11] To have that appreciation reciprocated by Carmilla as when she declares: "I have been in love with no one, and never shall...unless it should be with you"[12] is enough to soothe some of Laura's unease at the relationship.

The power that one lover has over another, no matter the gender(s) is difficult to depict—it might appear as soft sensuality—a kind of literary "fade to black" that evokes comforting feelings. Or it can be as obsessive and predatory as Carmilla appears to be when she says: "I live in you; and you would die for me..."[13] The power of desire is often messy, inappropriate, and not "woke," which Le Fanu is unafraid to depict.

I don't use the term "woke" dismissively. This unbridled passion in Carmilla's character certainly filled me with hope that as a lesbian feminist I would be able to create a more fully rounded lesbian vampire character for contemporary audiences. As an unexplained lassitude descends on Laura she remains faithful to her love. However, when Carmilla's nature is discovered and a cure is effected for Laura's diminishing health she is grateful, although her "satisfaction was changed to dismay, on discovering when she returns home that there were no tidings of Carmilla."[14] It is the earlier faithful, undiminished female devotion and desire, undimmed by lassitude, which I took to heart as I started writing *The Gilda Stories*.

---

11. Le Fanu, *Carmilla*, 80.
12. Le Fanu, *Carmilla*, 97.
13. Le Fanu, *Carmilla*, 97.
14. Le Fanu, *Carmilla*, 160.

Carmilla provided me with a door into two literary worlds I wanted to embrace: lesbian eroticism and vampire mythology. My goal was to translate the concept of Gothicism—with its own sexual undercurrents—into a form digestible by contemporary readers who were being asked to embrace a reshaped mythology that contrasted with the traditional presentation of vampires as white, upper class and male. In addition, I wished my central vampire characters to possess an obvious consciousness about culture at large, their sexuality, and their political circumstance.

I wrote and published my short story, *Caramelle*, in 2011[15], twenty years after the original publication of *The Gilda Stories* when I revisited the Le Fanu novella to touch base with the novel's origins. What I found in reading *Carmilla* this time was a resounding parallel with the "Underground Railroad" and the African Americans who used this network of abolitionists to escape enslavement. The tale is about those escaping and those who helped them rather than simply another story about Gilda. It provided an opportunity for me to write about the original Gilda, the bordello madam, apart from her subsequent namesake who is at the core of my novel. The result is an episode in what may be considered a prequel to *The Gilda Stories*.

Despite efforts by current conservatives to disavow the shame and harm of that peculiar institution many slave narratives have ripped off the outer skin of the festering wound which was enslavement. Several of the most famous are the Federal Writers Project[16]

15. Victoria Brownworth, ed., *From Where We Sit* (Philadelphia: Tiny Satchel Press, 2011).

16. Federal Writers Project, Library of Congress, 1936-1938.

which interviewed survivors; *Narrative of the Life of Frederick Douglass*,[17] a memoir; and *Incidents in the Life of a Slave Girl*,[18] a most startling memoir by Harriet Jacobs (using the name Linda Brent) that describes escaping the sexual predation of the plantation owner by hiding in an attic for seven years!

The mythic story of the escape of African Americans from enslavement has been told most frequently through the legendary life of Harriet Tubman,[19] who headed at least 13 missions leading African Americans from enslavement to freedom as well as working as a Union scout and spy and crusader for women's rights. And more recently, Colson Whitehead's Pulitzer Prize-winning novel, *The Underground Railroad*,[20] revisits that terrain through alternative history with speculative fiction elements.

The Le Fanu novella evoked the idea of women on the run and the way station which offered them relief before embarking on the next leg of their journey. As I was writing *Caramelle*, I kept hearing Tennessee Williams' Blanche DuBois saying that she has always "...depended on the kindness of strangers..."[21] The idea evoked so much of what I feel was vital to the success of the Underground Railroad specifically and to the survival of people

---

17. Continuously in print since published in 1845.

18. "Incidents in the Life of a Slave Girl," Linda Brent originally self-published in 1861 in Boston.

19. Harriet Tubman (aka Moses) is the subject of numerous literary studies both factual and fictionalized.

20. Colson Whitehead, *The Underground Railroad* (NYC: Doubleday, 2016).

21. Tennessee Williams, *A Street Car Named Desire* (NYC: Dramatists Play Service, 1997), 153.

under the oppression of a dominant culture, whether it's the institution of slavery or a fascistic government.

My hope is that *Carmilla* and *Caramelle* will remind us of several things: it was not so long ago that women's right to self-expression was completely defined and curtailed by a male-dominated culture. We should also remember that it doesn't take very much to turn the clock backward for women and others who've been oppressed. We see this goal reflected today on tee shirts featuring swastikas or slogans like "Her body/My choice," produced and sold by popular cultural figures.

We are also experiencing this currently in the political sphere where politicians gather votes to repeal women's rights to our own bodies, to dismantle voting rights legislation, as well as to deny due process for immigrants and access for those with disabilities.

Finally and most importantly, these stories should remind us that despite the monumental forces assembled against democratic principles, women, lesbians, immigrants, those with disabilities, and people of color have faced this type of oppression before. As in the past we still hold our freedom and our pleasure in our own strong hands. Hands made even stronger when holding on to the hands of others.

CARAMELLE JEWELLE GOMEZ

FOR J. SHERIDAN LE FANU

CARAMELLE

Looking back, it all seems both mysterious and natural and perhaps it was.

I remember watching my father, Solomon, scan the road outside of our small house for a sign. It was always uncertain whether he was more relieved when he discovered one or when he did not. He often invoked the name of the Lord either way, but he sometimes appeared too exhausted to remember further prayers. He was not a tall man, thinly built with fine bones that made his face seem delicate. But he always looked as if he had important jobs to do. Watching for the sign was one of them.

Before turning to me, he wiped his thin, dark hand over the tight nap of hair which capped his head. I looked away, quickly pretending to study my book on the table before me. Now, when I remember my father, it is those fleeting moments that bring his face to my mind most precisely. The look in his eyes—a mixture of anxiety, excitement, and love. Coiled inside of him was a fierceness that his wiry frame barely concealed.

His determination was a force like a storm unleashed or a river running down to the ocean; freedom was always his goal. He spoke of it to me and everyone who would listen so often that freedom became a tangible thing, a thing to taste like berry pie. And it became our name—Freeman—when we settled.

We'd come to live in Charlmont, Massachusetts, before my memory starts, but I do know the move followed my mother's passing to the other side. I must have still been in arms when she passed; I don't remember her at all, except, perhaps the feel of her cradling me. Despite that, I have come to associate her with the farm to which we fled. More precisely, I felt her presence most intensely whenever I was in the small barn where we kept the pigs, chickens, and our one horse.

That eeriness didn't worry me. In fact, I enjoyed the sense of warmth that rose from the pile of hay in the far corner of the barn and the deep quiet which sometimes settled gently over the drafty space. I liked to sit with the animals when Father had the men in our kitchen. The meetings, usually on Sunday, were much too full of tension for me. Mr. Leavitt and the other white men sat at our hard wood plank table as if they were in their own more refined parlours. They spoke in low tones that were, never-the-less, urgent.

We'd lived there for some years before I understood: our farm was a depot—a place where those, like my father and me, stopped on their way to freedom. No one ever actually said these words, but the succession of "cousins" who stayed with us in the years before I turned 14 was steady. Each would be called by the same name depending on the age. Men were called Cousin Simon, women were Cousin Delia, and children were Cousins Henrietta or John. I think Father decided to use the same names so as not to tax my childish memory.

Sometimes it became a source of a smile for Father and me. He'd look up say "Wonder if we'll have a cousin for dinner tonight?" And I'd say, "Yes, please. May we have them with jam?"

It was the purest joy to hear my father laugh out loud. He was not a grim man, but he was always contained. At the time I didn't use that word, of course, but it described the way he held his own counsel and parsed his words as if he wanted always to be prepared to respond properly and never be surprised into saying something too revealing or dangerous.

Once, when I was nine, I believe, I asked about our journey to the farm. I wanted to know how we'd come to be there, among the white people who were kind but so remote and strange I could never fit their words to the expressions on their faces. As we were sitting by the kitchen fire, he told the story speaking as if he were in a trance. It was then I understood our journey had been an escape.

"After your mother passed over, I don't know exactly what come over me. I couldn't watch you die like I'd watched your mother. She worked herself into the ground and then just let go." His voice choked but he went on.

"When she was gone not a single thing on that plantation stopped. The house kept on running like she'd never been there!

The only way I knew they knew your mother was gone was the misses sent us down some fruit—like we were going to have a party! And that was that. One night, I tied you to my back like I saw the women do in the fields. I threw a rag on my head and one of your mother's dresses over it all and walked away.

"I faced east then north, with you on my back; stole milk where I could. You were the quietest thing; not a sound from you when you were hungry. I worried about that, thinking maybe you were getting so little nourishment it was going to hurt you. But you were as strong as that horse out in that barn. I thought we'd die sometimes but I could feel the strength in you, feel it on my back and in those little hands holding on."

I later heard the stories of the life of slavery he'd left behind on the plantation. Mostly from the cousins who "visited." One whose skin was drawn so tight by the scars of the lash she could hardly bend over.

Another who walked with such a severe limp I wondered that he'd been able to cross the great distance from the world of slavery to our New England farm at all.

By the time I was fourteen it ceased feeling like a secret game and I understood the stark terror the cousins had endured to make the journey north. It was the same terror and grief that had driven my father to put on my mother's clothes and escape.

"We've got cousins tonight."

"With jam?"

"No, sugar pie. Cousin Delia and Cousin Henrietta be in tonight."

"Oh!"

With that I went to the area where I slept to be certain I'd not left a terrible mess. I was, by nature, quite neat; however, I was sometimes prone to leaving pieces of paper about when I was studying my books. I was determined to read and write as well as the white men who came to meetings at our house on Sundays. I believe I felt I might be less lonely if I could write things down. Ever since Father had given me the book of poems by Phillis Wheatley, I knew I was doing something valuable.

"O, Thou bright jewel in my aim I strive To comprehend thee." As we finished dinner, my father, as he often did, tossed a quote in the air for me to identify.

"That's easy, Father, Phillis Wheatley!"

How could I dwell on loneliness when words and love surrounded me? But sometimes there it was, sitting at the foot of my bed; which is perhaps why I liked the barn. It was never lonely there.

I heard the buckboard on the road before Father did. His hearing was getting thinner each year, which he would never admit, of course. Mr. Leavitt, pale in the dim light thrown by the lantern at his side, helped Cousin Delia down first. She was tall and fair-skinned, almost as pale as Mr. Leavitt. She wore her head wrap drawn tightly down across her brow, shadowing her eyes. Her bones seemed to almost pierce the fabric of her cloak, not unexpected given the harsh journey they'd taken. The flight from the South to the North was hardly a nutritious one.

Cousin Delia reached up to lift her daughter down before Mr. Leavitt could and the sinewy strength of her arms and back were evident despite her meager frame. Cousin Henrietta was almost as tall as her mother and just as pale. She could have been 11 or 16; it was difficult to tell in the dim light. Mr. Leavitt handed my father a small satchel, barely said good night, and climbed back up on the seat of his buckboard.

That was unusual; Mr. Leavitt's way was shy but regular. He'd come in to settle his charges, often have a cup of cider to be neighborly and then promise to return with more "victuals." That meant he'd return with the guide for the next aspect of our cousins' journey. Tonight, he turned away looking exhausted, as if he'd not slept in days. I suppose when he came on Sunday, we'd hear more of what might be going on outside our little town.

"Goodnight to you, sir." Mr. Leavitt said.

We turned to our charges and offered a small snack.

"We kinda tired suh. If you don't mind, we'd like to...."

"I understand, Cousin. No tea?"

"Naw."

I couldn't see her eyes well, but they didn't look tired at all.

Her voice didn't seem as weak as her words, but I couldn't tell; so, I turned to her daughter. She stared back at me with coal black eyes that were full of fear. That made more sense than the sound of her mother's voice, so I took her hand and led her to the space she and her mother would occupy until it was time for them to move north.

Once they were settled in, Father rolled back his blanket so I could sleep in his bed in the narrow alcove; then he slid the curtain across on the thick branch which rested at the top of the wall. He checked the bolt across the door and settled on a pallet by the stove. I loved the sound of Father nestling into the wool-covered hay; it reminded me of the barn.

Usually, I'd lie awake imagining what news the new cousins might share the next day. This time my eyelids fell shut almost before I'd settled. And then it was morning.

Father was outside at the pump running water over his head and face, and the kettle was almost at the boil on the stove. There was no sound from my room. He said Cousin Delia had asked they not be disturbed; they might sleep through the day. I put a piece of ham bone in a pot at the back of the stove then worked outside gathering greens and then eggs from the barn. Father took the horse over to the Fahey farm to help with their tilling, and I tried not to listen at the door to my room. I truly wanted to meet Cousin Henrietta.

Near dusk, done with my chores, I ran water over my head like Father always did and I loved the way it soaked my collar, even though I knew Father would not be pleased. No one could resist the smell of my stew, so I pulled dishes out and set them on our small table. I decided to use our cloth napkins even though it wasn't Sunday. I'd have to wash them before the men came for their meeting but I didn't mind; I wanted the cousins to feel welcome.

Cousin Delia stood in the doorway. It felt like she towered over me although she wasn't really much taller than I was. I'd seen many different colours of coloured people since we'd had the visiting cousins, but something about this Delia was unlike anyone I'd ever met. Coolness rolled off of her like fog rising from the cranberry bog. I smiled, though, and asked if she wanted tea.

"Yes, that be nice…uh…?"

"Elisabeth," I provided. Father had given me my mother's name after she passed.

Cousin Delia looked at me as if we were really related and said, "How fortunate."

I thought that was an interesting response, but people on the railroad often had an odd relationship to words, to space, to everything. It was like they were trying to understand the world when they had only been living in it underwater. Everything is familiar but distorted; nothing comes easily.

"Mama?"

Cousin Henrietta stood behind her mother. Her eyes were the same dark pools, but I could see a smile lurking there. This was my favorite thing…to learn who the children were before they were gone, back onto the road; since there really wasn't any train. Then for days I'd imagine the mysterious places they might have landed—New York or Canada. I always thought of them as having tea somewhere nice and sunny and cool.

The kettle came to a boil, and I made tea for them both in our old, chipped pot, and decided to wait for Father to have mine. Before he returned, Cousin Delia announced she wanted to go out for a walk. I told her Father would advise against it and she sat back in her chair as if he'd actually spoken.

"Well then…" she said, indecision filling the air.

"Father will be home soon and we'll have supper."

They were silent. Cousin Henrietta smiled, though.

"I'm going out to the barn to set the hay for when Father comes back with the horse. You want to come?" I said to her.

"Oh yes, please."

I could tell her mother wanted to say no but held back.

"Come along, Cousin Henrietta," I said as I took her hand. I was relieved to be out of the house, which seemed to fill up with her mother's anxiety. I didn't know if this was the natural state of mothers since I'd not fully known mine, but it was a distinctly unpleasant feeling.

"My name is Caramelle."

"You mustn't say that."

"Well, it is, and I don't like being called something else."

Once we were inside, I shut the barn door like always and she looked startled.

"Why'd you do that?"

"You're supposed to shut the barn door so there's no coming and going."

Something about that made her giggle and then me too. We laughed until we fell down into the pile of hay and the chickens cackled around us. We lay there smiling at the beams and tackle hanging above us. It was the same peacefulness that I always enjoyed but somehow made richer by Caramelle being here.

"I remember this place."

"How can you remember a place you've never been?" I asked.

"Through dreams, silly!" Caramelle laughed again which took the edge off her words.

She watched me wield the pitchfork, tossing the hay over into the horse stall, and smiled like it was the most charming entertainment.

"Where have you traveled from?" I knew I wasn't to ask but I couldn't stop myself.

"I ain't supposed to say."

Then she looked at the closed door and nestled into the hay like she was totally at home.

"Maryland."

"Didn't they already pass emancipation? That's what the white men told Father!!"

"Yes, but we had to get on the road anyway."

"Oh?"

"I tell you the story 'cause I'm so tired from carrying it all by myself. Mama, she knows, but she don't talk. You can see that, can't ya?"

That seemed for sure. Cousin Delia hadn't spoken more than ten words in the ten hours she'd been in our little house.

"A man, a friend of the massa, used to come all the time and bother me." Cousin Henrietta's, I mean Caramelle's eyes got even darker as she spoke.

"He was always fearsome cold. And he look at folks like they weren't really there. One night he...he turn into something. He locked us in the room then he turn me into something."

"I don't understand."

"I can't explain exactly but Mother too. He did it to her too."

"What about your daddy? Didn't he...?"

"Massa were my daddy."

I stopped pitching the hay then and looked at the girl who was curled up before me. She was both innocent and old at the same time. I knew the taste for cruelty that infected slave owners, but I hate that it had touched Caramelle.

"Do you want to see the secret place?" I asked. I might have to show it to them soon anyway, but this seemed a good time.

I opened the gate to the stall and dug the pitchfork around under the hay until I found the seam in the wood floor.

"See here." I pried until the hatch opened and revealed the trough we'd dug into the ground below. It was lined with hay and a blanket but was still not the most inviting accommodation. We'd only used it once when a relentless bounty hunter had followed some cousins almost to our door. But that had been more than a year ago and the news was that the war was almost over.

"Let's get in!" Caramelle cried with excitement.

I'd once slipped into the little cubbyhole just to understand what it felt like to hide there. It was musty and dark and at the same time like a cocoon, ready to release its magical creature.

I tipped the hatch back and Caramelle dropped into the hole as if she'd been invited into a grand salon. I looked at the closed barn door then slid down beside her. It could not have been more than four feet by six feet and was about four feet deep. I closed the hatch over us and felt a few sprigs of hay drift through the cracks.

Caramelle started to giggle and put her arm around me, wriggled in close and whispered in my ear: "Can I tell you the rest of the story?"

I couldn't imagine what more there would be.

"He tried to take me and Mama from Massa Harriwell, that 'twere his name, but the misses didn't want to let us go since she loved my mama's hands. Mama used to work in the kitchen, but she had a great way with massaging when people had aches and pains. Did you notice her hands?"

I had, indeed, noticed the strength of her hands and the muscles that lined her arms last night. It seemed unusual for someone so slight.

"Well, he was determined and Massa Harriwell finally give us up, not for cheap though."

"Once we was on the road that man kept messing with me and one night Mama just got mad and killed him."

"Killed him?"

"Yeah. She pick up the small hatchet she keep in her things and took off his head. She said that was the only thing to do. But that we really had to run now. She said his people was gonna be mad and we had to get north."

The chill that had surrounded her mother now also emanated from Caramelle. I hadn't noticed that before. Or maybe in remembering the death of her tormentor the fit of emotion had made her temperature drop. My own bones were suddenly taken with a winter frost.

"We been traveling ever since, trying to figure out how to live since he used to take care of that."

"Take care of what?"

"We better go, ain't your papa coming home soon?" Caramelle asked abruptly.

"Yes," I said, more confused than when the story was started. I understood about white men messing with girls. I understood about escaping and sometimes killing. That's why there was a war, and the people who met with my father tried to talk in low tones so I wouldn't hear about dying, but I did.

Caramelle and I pushed open the hatch together and climbed out, brushing straw from our clothes. I realized then that I wanted to give her something new to wear. Her own clothes were caked with mud and dark stains. It seemed like she should be starting a new life with new clothes. I determined then to sew something for her.

It was a funny dinner; the cousins seemed to eat very little if anything. Father was almost jovial and I kept thinking it was because of Caramelle's mama. She had snuck out the house while we were in the barn. I could tell because she had brambles on her skirt but her walk had done her good. She looked less haggard and even laughed when Father told her stories.

We were up later than usual talking when she asked Father if she could rub his shoulders. He was startled, then Caramelle said, "The missus really 'preciated Mama's shoulder rub. You should, I'm telling you!"

Father laughed saying, "Well with a recommendation like that from our little cousin how can I say no?"

With that he sent me and Caramelle to bed and Cousin Delia rubbed my Father's shoulders with those strong hands of hers, hands that had wielded an ax and took a man's head off.

I didn't think I could sleep knowing that, but I barely lay down before it felt like it was morning.

Caramelle and her mama kept to the room 'til later. Father said Cousin Delia had explained that she and her daughter suffered from an eye disorder that made bright light hard on them. That made me feel terrible. But I went about my chores quietly and even did my studying early so I'd be free to enjoy Caramelle when she finally emerged. It did give me a chance to think about what kind of dress I'd be making. I'd asked Father and he agreed it would be a neighbourly thing to do. He'd ask Mrs. Leavitt to pick out a bolt of cloth for it when she went into town.

Father didn't like going to town much, especially to do things like go to the dry goods store. Even though Mr. Leavitt and the white men who'd helped us and were fierce believers in freedom sometimes folks in town weren't sure what they believed. If Father was delivering hay or coming to fix something, all was fine. But if we went into town for stores or household goods. shopkeepers didn't seem to know what to do with us. It was like they'd never imagined that coloured people made soap or dresses or liked tea. That made us too much like them and they'd have to examine not just what was in their heads but what was in their hearts about coloured people.

"Tell more about what you spoke of yesterday...learning to..."

"Mama don't want us talking about that."

"She didn't want me to know your name is Caramelle either."

I'd come to love the sound of her name. It reminded me of something soft and warm, which was how she'd felt when she curled around me under the floorboards in the horse stall. It was something I don't think I'd ever experienced before that moment.

"Come on; let's go under the horse stall where no one can hear us!"

She was as eager as I and we lay together like I'd seen puppies do under their mother's belly after drinking their fill. But this was different. A scent of coolness misted her skin yet her dark eyes burned hot. Where she touched me, I felt warm and something else. It was as if she were touching not just my skin but my blood and bones too. Like her mother's, Caramelle's hands were uncommonly strong. I was pleased by that because I always hated the idea that girls were weaker than boys.

I'd heard Father talking to Mr. Leavitt and knew my ability to chop kindling was not hampered by what Mr. Leavitt referred to in his own sons as a "lazy streak wide as the Deerfield River."

I leaned in closer and absorbed the sensation of being held with the unusual strength of Caramelle and barely heard her story because of the joy flowing through my body.

"I beg your pardon?"

"You silly thing!" Caramelle said laughing. "You're not falling asleep, are you?"

"No, not at all. Please go on."

"We met her on the road. We were ragged with hunger and exhaustion. She just stepped out of the dark and fed us. She was tracking us and that ain't so easy because we move pretty near fast as a ...well fast."

"Can we run together sometime in the woods to the back?"

"If Mama says."

I didn't want to hold out hope since Caramelle's mother, despite her almost total silence, managed to convey a sense that she would not approve of much that Caramelle and I would want to do.

"So, her and Mama talked mostly quiet-like 'til Mama said something and the other one's voice got real hard and scared me. But then she was soft again; I think she told Mama things about how we could make it north without the slavecatchers gettin' us. Then she rubbed my face, smiled, and leaned down to kiss me I figured. Instead she whispered, 'You see trouble call me, you hear gal?' I think that's what she said anyway. That's when I ask my mama what her name was 'cause I wondered how I was gonna call her if I didn't know her name.

"I ain't seen a smile like that since Mama...since he changed Mama. Then Gilda, that was what Mama said her name was, just disappeared like she'd come...into the dark." Caramelle stopped abruptly.

"Gracious! You think she was an escaped slave?"

"I don't think so. She walked like...I don't know...just different. And she talked different too. More like you. And she was wearing men's breeches! I knew she was a woman though, so did Mama."

I could see Caramelle was starting to feel low, so I didn't push her. I supposed her mother didn't want her to be sad; that's why she forbade her talking about these things.

The next day Caramelle rose shortly before her mother as if she was as eager as I to enjoy each other's company. She almost caught me as I basted a piece of the fabric Father had brought home. He'd convinced me to make an apron not a dress; he said our cousins wouldn't be staying long enough for such a project.

I'd just finished adding a bit of grosgrain ribbon I had left from a dress I'd made for myself and all that remained was to hem the bottom. I popped the almost completed gift under my own apron when Caramelle appeared in the doorway. Her dark eyes sparkled with excitement.

"Come, let me redo your hair."

"Mama gonna do it."

"No, please let me."

I took the brush down from behind the one mirror we had hanging by the reading table and had Caramelle sit between my legs on the floor where I used to sit when Father combed my hair.

Caramelle's hair was a sandy brown colour, very soft; and not nearly as tangled as mine gets when I sleep. I brushed gently and redid each part neatly so it looked exactly as it had before. I loved the feel of it in my hands. I don't know why, but just before I started braiding, I leaned down and kissed the center part where the sweetness of her scalp showed through.

Caramelle sighed deeply and sat very still as I finished the rows of braids that ran across the crown of her head. I slipped a small piece of the leftover ribbon from my apron and tied the ends of the rows together at the base of her head, making a tiny bow.

"Ohhh! I never had a bow before!" Caramelle said touching the piece of fabric gently as if she could see it with her fingers.

"Look Mama," Caramelle said. Without turning, she'd clearly heard her mother step into the doorway. I was startled since there is a huge squeak in the board just before the door which I had to carefully avoid when I got up in the middle of the night if I didn't want to wake Father.

"I see."

Her mother's voice was the saddest sound. She looked around the room as if noting it for the first time and it seemed as if she'd cry but no tears came. Caramelle jumped up and threw herself into her mother's arms.

My heart sunk at that sight, because it was a vibrant reminder that Caramelle belonged to her mother and they would both be gone soon. I went to the stove to stoke the fire so the stew cooking would be done when Father arrived. I slipped the apron under the bedding and went back to the stove keeping my back to the image of Caramelle and her mother although I would always see it.

"Mama, we got to go move hay in the barn now."

"Miss Elisabeth don't need you underfoot while she doin' her work, child."

"Mama, I help. You know I'm strong."

"Cousin Delia, I love having Car...Cousin Henrietta with me. Please?"

"Alright."

The sound of defeat again seemed to hang over her as she sank down into the chair where I'd been combing Caramelle's hair.

We tried not to hurry out to the barn, but our feet did not obey. Father would be home soon, and we both knew we had little time left together. Mr. Leavitt would send someone to take them north at any moment.

"Can we…"

I had the floorboard pried up and lowered myself before Caramelle could finish asking.

"You know why we got to go all the way to Canada."

"The slave catcher?"

"Naw, Mama say since she killed that man his people is coming after us."

"The master?"

"Ain't him. It's the ones that change people like he did me and Mama."

"I don't know what you mean."

"I can't say exactly, except we ain't like we used to be…the daylight is hard on us and we have to…"

Here she stopped and I almost wanted her to stay silent. Something in her voice made me afraid. Through the slats of the floor, a little lamplight filtered down to our hiding place floating on the bits of hay. But her golden arms tight against the brown of mine made my heart jump to my throat; and I wanted to feel her breath on my neck as she spoke.

"That devilish man took our lives. First, he was messing with me, which Mama said was hateful. Then he took our lives."

"What does that mean?"

"He…he made it so we have to drink blood to stay alive."

Caramelle said it in that childlike voice that I'd come to love but the chill of it swept over me. She sensed it and held me closer.

"Please don't be afraid. I promise I won't hurt you."

"I never thought you would, Caramelle. I just don't understand what you're saying."

"There's some folks that...this is the way they live. Mostly they mean and evil like the one who took us. Kind of like the massa but worse 'cause they don't never die."

I wanted to laugh but I couldn't. Suddenly I felt too big for the little space below the floorboards and Caramelle's arms were so tight around me I couldn't move.

"Miss Gilda told Mama everything. That made her feel better for a while, but she's still really scared the others are coming after her. You ain't supposed to kill the one who..."

Caramelle stopped as if she couldn't bear to talk about it anymore, and I nestled in closer to assure her I wasn't afraid and because it felt so good to have her body close to mine.

"Want me to show you something? I promise it won't change you." "Yes," I said, although the breath gathered in my chest and almost choked off the word. My heart pounded with both fear and anticipation. Caramelle leaned up on one elbow and pressed her mouth to mine.

It was gentle at first and, since I'd never had such a kiss, my first response was to be startled. Caramelle held on to my shoulders and her lips were insistent on mine until she said:

"Yes?"

"Yes," I answered and then let the warmth of her mouth spread through me. I kissed back and the heat became a fire that I felt down to the bottom of my stomach then beyond. I could barely breathe but was desperate to keep her mouth on mine. I moaned in sadness as her mouth slipped away, then to my cheek and down to my neck. The heat of her lips on my skin was almost unbearable. I could feel the stirring inside me that sometimes came when I had dreams, and I wanted only that she not stop.

I felt a small sharpness at my neck where she kissed me again and I felt as if I was falling into a hole—except I was already in a hole. Caramelle's lips were the only thing I understood at that moment and that she was taking my blood. But I trusted her. She was looking inside my mind or my heart, I could feel that. When she pulled back, she looked me in the eye and said, "Now you'll always be a part of me just as you wanted."

My eyes were out of focus and I felt as if the horse that usually occupied the stall above was standing directly on me.

"Rest. You'll be fine in just a moment, I promise. I didn't take much."

"Much?"

"That was one of the things that Miss Gilda taught me and Mama. That nasty man just liked to kill folks but Miss Gilda said we don't have to.

I must have drifted off then, but I awoke to Father calling my name. His voice had a slight tinge of anxiety, and I realized it must have gotten late.

"We have to hurry. Father doesn't like me to play under here anymore."

Caramelle looked at me carefully as if to make sure I was not ill- affected by our secret moment.

"Now I'll always be with you." I said with a smile to reassure her. I did feel a little light headed but nothing else seemed out of order; except I could not stop smiling at Caramelle, nor she at me.

"I'm sorry Father, we were just ..." as we greeted him in the yard.

Caramelle's mother snatched her from my side.

"Mama!" Caramelle protested.

"Elisabeth, you gave our cousin Delia a scare. She didn't know where you were."

"I do apologize Cousin Delia. We wandered off as I was telling Cousin Henrietta all my stories."

"You didn't fall asleep out there in those woods, did ya?" There was a hint of terror in Cousin Delia's voice.

"No, Cousin. Time just got away from us. I apologize."

"There. All's well that ends well," Father said.

"William Shakespeare, 1604," I answered with more pride because Caramelle could witness my scholarship.

I could tell Father wasn't very angry because he'd played our game of throwing titles and quotations from texts I'd been studying and he beamed when I got it right.

"What's that?" Caramelle asked.

"Let's have our last night together and Elisabeth, who loves to tell stories so much, will tell you all about William Shakespeare."

I was extremely sad and happy at the same time. I could already feel how I missed Caramelle, but I was also relieved that she would be taken north out of harm's way...slave catchers or the family of the evil man.

"I'll be sorry to see you leave us cousins," Father said. His voice made me understand that he was as lonely in this life as I sometimes was.

"There's been a bit of activity lately so we're sorry for the delay. But tomorrow evening you'll be on your way and safe and sound before you know it."

"Mama, I feel safe here."

"I know, gal, but you can see we ain't. And if we stay they won't be neither."

"I believe Elisabeth has a little gift she made for you, Cousin. We want you to always remember us."

I reluctantly pulled the apron from beneath the covers on Father's bed. It wasn't completely finished and worse, when it was done I knew they were gone for sure.

"I just have a few more stitches...if you want it..."

Caramelle squealed with joy as she held the little apron to her heart. We sat talking about the road, what Father could tell them about the way to Canada; things he'd heard from Mr. Leavitt. I finished the hem and turning over the ends of the apron strings, and Caramelle tried it on.

"I'm sorry there wasn't time to make you a new dress."

"Oh, this is much better for travelling! And if I ever get a new dress, I'll make sure it matches this pretty colour."

For the first time Caramelle's mother's face was washed with a full and brilliant smile.

The soft knock on our door startled us as if it had been the crack of a cannon ball. A visitor at this hour was rare unless there was some trouble, and the conductor wasn't due until tomorrow. The smile on Cousin Delia's face slid away, replaced with a look of terror and then a fierceness I'd never seen.

"Mr. Freeman?"

Father was surprised to hear his name; everyone in town just called him by his Christian name, except the Quakers, who called everyone mister and miss. He opened the door more puzzled than afraid. A remarkable woman stood there in men's breeches and jacket with a hat in her hand.

At first, I thought she was white, her skin was fair and almost translucent, much like Cousin Delia's but even more so. Yet around the edges I could see an almost bronze tone beneath her skin that told me she was a mulatto. And I could tell who it was by the catch of Caramelle's breath.

"Mr. Freeman, I apologize for the lateness of the hour, but may I come in?"

"Of course," Father said before Cousin Delia could say anything, although it was clear she had intended to protest.

"Ah, my cousins...good." "May I ask..."

"Of course, again I apologize, Mr. Freeman for interrupting your final evening but it's impossible for them to stay here another minute."

I rushed to Caramelle's side and grabbed her hand, which was as cold as the river in winter. She clutched my little apron in her other hand as if it was the gold.

"What do you want with us?" Cousin Delia sputtered.

"I want only to protect you. You know they are after you."

"Slave catchers...close?" Father was immediately suspicious.

"Worse," she answered quickly.

"Madam," my father said sternly, "I assure you there is no worse than a slave catcher."

"There is a bounty on their heads, and the return of their bodies would be just as rewarding." Cousin Delia flinched as the words fell on her.

"Bounty? Why?"

"I'm afraid we don't have time for the full story. Cousin, tell them it is true so we may make our way before it's too late. Or do you wish to see the blood of your hosts shed as well?"

As hard as I tried to hold them back, tears started to fall because I couldn't bear to be separated from Caramelle. I hoped for the briefest moment she and her mother might take me with them. Caramelle straightened beside me and stopped clutching the apron.

"Elisabeth please stop cryin'," Father said gently.

Caramelle tried to smile as she said, "Mama, you knows we got to go with Miss Gilda."

"You know each other then?" Father was a bit relieved although still puzzled.

"I hate leavin' you, Elisabeth, but she right," Caramelle's voice was sweet but firm as if she knew she had to make the decision for her mother, who seemed frozen by her alarm.

"But where will you go? I..." the words evaporated before I could say them. Not knowing where Caramelle would be seemed like a life much too bleak to comprehend.

"Dear Elisabeth, you really are true aren't you?" the woman Gilda said to me and smiled her sincerity. "You mustn't be sad. I've a wonderful place for our cousins and it's perfect! Do you know why?"

"No." I tried to stop sniffling and be as grown up as my dear friend to whom I was still clinging.

"Well, it's perfect because it has the same name as she does. So deep in your heart you'll always know where she is."

The mystery was too opaque and my confusion was apparent.

"Can we see each other again?"

"That is possible."

Here Miss Gilda also looked sad, "If so, it will not be for a long time. But you mustn't worry."

Her voice remained soft and even. It soothed the air in the room which was rustling with anxiety.

"Are you ready?"

Fear held Cousin Delia locked in stillness.

"Even Caramelle has learned more quickly than you!" Miss Gilda's voice remained soft but carried a hard edge that was chilling. "Take only what you need and leave something in exchange. You will be able to live and not like the others. You must believe me."

Cousin Delia's stillness broke and she turned back to look at Father and me, then stepped back to the hook to take her cloak.

"We'll leave immediately and make a wide circle, leading them away from this farm, then head north. Once we're in another territory you'll be safe."

"How can you be sure?" Father asked, not really clear what he was asking.

"I've seen this before. The bounty will be void as long as they don't return to this territory.

"All right cousins. Let me pack up some of that meat that was in the stew and the rest of the bread."

"That won't be necessary," Miss Gilda said, adding quickly, "I've nourishment hidden along the route."

"You've been a true cousin Mr. Freeman," Cousin Delia finally said, "We thank you and Miss Elisabeth for your kindness."

Caramelle threw her arms around my neck and kissed me where she had taken my blood and whispered, "I left something in exchange."

Miss Gilda watched us closely all the while speaking in a soft, even voice that was almost mesmerizing.

"No one should follow. If anyone asks you will have no recollection of us. I've already communicated with Mr. Leavitt, so there's no need to speak with him. All's well that ends well, eh?" With that she smiled at me and put her arms around Cousin Delia and Caramelle, sweeping them out the door into the night.

That was 15 years ago. Father died several years later, as if the knowledge that freedom had finally come it to our people allowed him to rest. I've been teaching the coloured children and doing some writing. I want to be certain that the memory of the cousins we sheltered doesn't fade inextricably, and that the heartless lives they fled and the bravery of their flight is remembered at least in print.

I like to tell the children about my dear father who was not too afraid to wear women's clothes to find our way to freedom. And I related the story of a cousin who'd swum across a river with her ill mother clinging to her back and the cousin who walked 100 miles to freedom using only the stars to guide his small feet and the many other tales of strength I'd heard from our cousins. This was the kind of resolve I knew they needed to hear in order to find their own. In some ways the end of slavery made it even more important for the children to understand their power. They are alone in a world that does not care for them.

After so many years in this small New England town, I hesitate to leave my charges behind. However, I have begun to feel blossoming inside me the urge to see other parts of the world. I don't know from whence it came but I no longer have anything to tie me to this place. The uncommon peace that lies over that drafty barn continues to engage and amaze me, although I no longer imagine my mother is there.

The pull to move on is most irresistible, as if the Underground Railroad car has stopped at this depot just for me. Although I haven't ever travelled, I've settled on an idea—Canada. After all of the cousins who were making their way north, it feels like somewhere I'd like to see for myself.

I sometimes hear a whisper: "I left something in exchange." After her hasty departure, I had searched my bed and desk and the barn but found nothing that was not as I'd left it. Soon the memory of them evaporated as if it slipped away from my mind like a whisp of smoke. Now I wonder if this urge is the mysterious something left behind for me.

My mind is made up, so I give the house back to Mr. Leavitt. In an old satchel, I pack my two dresses, a few other garments, my brush, sewing needles, scissors along with the coins I've been saving and those Mr. Leavitt gifted me.

For no reason I can identify a place keeps surfacing in my mind. I'm going to make my way to a town in Canada called Caramelle City.

CARMILLA   J. SHERIDAN LE FANU

PROLOGUE

Upon a paper attached to the Narrative which follows, Doctor
Hesselius has written a rather elaborate note, which he
accompanies with a reference to his Essay on the strange subject
which the MS. illuminates.

This mysterious subject he treats, in that Essay, with his usual
learning and acumen, and with remarkable directness and con-
densation. It will form but one volume of the series of that extraordinary man's collected papers.

As I publish the case, in this volume, simply to interest the
"laity," I shall forestal the intelligent lady, who relates it, in nothing; and, after due consideration, I have determined, therefore,
to abstain from presenting any *précis* of the learned Doctor's
reasoning, or extract from his statement on a subject which he

describes as "involving, not improbably, some of the profoundest arcana of our dual existence, and its intermediates."

I was anxious, on discovering this paper, to reopen the correspondence commenced by Doctor Hesselius, so many years before, with a person so clever and careful as his informant seems to have been. Much to my regret, however, I found that she had died in the interval.

She, probably, could have added little to the Narrative which she communicates in the following pages, with, so far as I can pronounce, such conscientious particularity.

CHAPTER I.

AN EARLY FRIGHT.

In Styria, we, though by no means magnificent people, inhabit a castle, or schloss. A small income, in that part of the world, goes a great way. Eight or nine hundred a year does wonders. Scantily enough ours would have answered among wealthy people at home. My father is English, and I bear an English name, although I never saw England. But here, in this lonely and primitive place, where everything is so marvelously cheap, I really don't see how ever so much more money would at all materially add to our comforts, or even luxuries.

My father was in the Austrian service, and retired upon a pension and his patrimony, and purchased this feudal residence, and the small estate on which it stands, a bargain.

Nothing can be more picturesque or solitary. It stands on a slight eminence in a forest. The road, very old and narrow, passes in front of its drawbridge, never raised in my time, and its moat, stocked with perch, and sailed over by many swans, and floating on its surface white fleets of water-lilies.

Over all this the schloss shows its many-windowed front; its towers, and its Gothic chapel.

The forest opens in an irregular and very picturesque glade before its gate, and at the right a steep Gothic bridge carries the road over a stream that winds in deep shadow through the wood.

I have said that this is a very lonely place. Judge whether I say truth. Looking from the hall door towards the road, the forest in which our castle stands extends fifteen miles to the right, and twelve to the left. The nearest inhabited village is about seven of your English miles to the left. The nearest inhabited schloss of any historic associations, is that of old General Spielsdorf, nearly twenty miles away to the right.

I have said "the nearest *inhabited* village," because there is, only three miles westward, that is to say in the direction of General Spielsdorf's schloss, a ruined village, with its quaint little church, now roofless, in the aisle of which are the moldering tombs of the proud family of Karnstein, now extinct, who once owned the equally desolate chateau which, in the thick of the forest, overlooks the silent ruins of the town.

Respecting the cause of the desertion of this striking and melancholy spot, there is a legend which I shall relate to you another time.

I must tell you now, how very small is the party who constitute the inhabitants of our castle. I don't include servants, or those dependents who occupy rooms in the buildings attached to the schloss. Listen, and wonder! My father, who is the kindest man on earth, but growing old; and I, at the date of my story, only nineteen. Eight years have passed since then. I and my father constituted the family at the schloss. My mother, a Styrian lady, died in my infancy, but I had a good-natured governess, who had been with me from, I might almost say, my infancy. I could not remember the time when her fat, benignant face was not a familiar picture in my memory. This was Madame Perrodon, a native of Berne, whose care and good nature now in part supplied to me the loss of my mother, whom I do not even remember, so early I lost her. She made a third at our little dinner party. There was a fourth, Mademoiselle De Lafontaine, a lady such as you term, I believe, a "finishing governess." She spoke French and German, Madame Perrodon French and broken English, to which my father and I added English, which, partly to prevent its becoming a lost language among us, and partly from patriotic motives, we spoke every day. The consequence was a Babel, at which strangers used to laugh, and which I shall make no attempt to reproduce in this narrative. And there were two or three young lady friends besides, pretty nearly of my own age, who were occasional visitors, for longer or shorter terms; and these visits I sometimes returned.

These were our regular social resources; but of course there were chance visits from "neighbors" of only five or six leagues' distance. My life was, notwithstanding, rather a solitary one, I can assure you.

My gouvernantes had just so much control over me as you might conjecture such sage persons would have in the case of a rather spoiled girl, whose only parent allowed her pretty nearly her own way in everything.

The first occurrence in my existence, which produced a terrible impression upon my mind, which, in fact, never has been effaced, was one of the very earliest incidents of my life which I can recollect. Some people will think it so trifling that it should not be recorded here. You will see, however, by-and-by, why I mention it. The nursery, as it was called, though I had it all to myself, was a large room in the upper story of the castle, with a steep oak roof. I can't have been more than six years old, when one night I awoke, and looking round the room from my bed, failed to see the nursery-maid. Neither was my nurse there; and I thought myself alone. I was not frightened, for I was one of those happy children who are studiously kept in ignorance of ghost stories, of fairy tales, and of all such lore as makes us cover up our heads when the door creaks suddenly, or the flicker of an expiring candle makes the shadow of a bedpost dance upon the wall, nearer to our faces. I was vexed and insulted at finding myself, as I conceived, neglected, and I began to whimper, preparatory to a hearty bout of roaring; when to my surprise, I saw a solemn, but very pretty face looking at me from the side of the bed. It was that of a young lady who was kneeling, with her hands under the coverlet. I looked at her with a kind of pleased wonder, and ceased whimpering. She caressed me with her hands, and lay down beside me on the bed, and drew me towards her, smiling; I felt immediately delightfully soothed, and fell asleep again. I was wakened by a sensation as if two needles ran into my breast very deep at the same moment, and I cried loudly. The lady started back, with her eyes fixed on me, and then slipped down upon the floor, and, as I thought, hid herself under the bed.

I was now for the first time frightened, and I yelled with all my might and main. Nurse, nursery-maid, housekeeper, all came running in, and hearing my story, they made light of it, soothing me all they could meanwhile. But, child as I was, I could perceive that their faces were pale with an unwonted look of anxiety, and I saw them look under the bed, and about the room, and peep under tables and pluck open cupboards; and the housekeeper whispered to the nurse: "Lay your hand along that hollow in the bed; some-one *did* lie there, so sure as you did not; the place is still warm."

I remember the nursery-maid petting me, and all three examining my chest, where I told them I felt the puncture, and pronouncing that there was no sign visible that any such thing had happened to me.

The housekeeper and the two other servants who were in charge of the nursery, remained sitting up all night; and from that time a servant always sat up in the nursery until I was about fourteen.

I was very nervous for a long time after this. A doctor was called in, he was pallid and elderly. How well I remember his long saturnine face, slightly pitted with small-pox, and his chestnut wig. For a good while, every second day, he came and gave me medicine, which of course I hated.

The morning after I saw this apparition I was in a state of terror, and could not bear to be left alone, daylight though it was, for a moment.

I remember my father coming up and standing at the bedside, and talking cheerfully, and asking the nurse a number of questions, and laughing very heartily at one of the answers; and patting me on the shoulder, and kissing me, and telling me not to be frightened, that it was nothing but a dream and could not hurt me.

But I was not comforted, for I knew the visit of the strange woman was *not* a dream; and I was *awfully* frightened.

I was a little consoled by the nursery-maid's assuring me that it was she who had come and looked at me, and lain down beside me in the bed, and that I must have been half-dreaming not to have known her face. But this, though supported by the nurse, did not quite satisfy me.

I remember, in the course of that day, a venerable old man, in a black cassock, coming into the room with the nurse and house-keeper, and talking a little to them, and very kindly to me; his face was very sweet and gentle, and he told me they were going to pray, and joined my hands together, and desired me to say, softly, while they were praying, "Lord, hear all good prayers for us, for Jesus' sake." I think these were the very words, for I often repeated them to myself, and my nurse used for years to make me say them in my prayers.

I remember so well the thoughtful sweet face of that white-haired old man, in his black cassock, as he stood in that rude, lofty, brown room, with the clumsy furniture of a fashion three hundred years old, about him, and the scanty light entering its shadowy atmosphere through the small lattice. He kneeled, and the three women with him, and he prayed aloud with an earnest quavering voice for, what appeared to me, a long time. I forget all my life preceding that event, and for some time after it is all obscure also; but the scenes I have just described stand out vivid as the isolated pictures of the phantasmagoria surrounded by darkness.

CHAPTER II.

A GUEST

I am now going to tell you something so strange that it will require all your faith in my veracity to believe my story. It is not only true, nevertheless, but truth of which I have been an eyewitness.

It was a sweet summer evening, and my father asked me, as he sometimes did, to take a little ramble with him along that beautiful forest vista which I have mentioned as lying in front of the schloss.

"General Spielsdorf cannot come to us so soon as I had hoped," said my father, as we pursued our walk.

He was to have paid us a visit of some weeks, and we had expected his arrival next day. He was to have brought with him a young lady, his niece and ward, Mademoiselle Rheinfeldt, whom I had never seen, but whom I had heard described as a very charming girl, and in whose society I had promised myself many happy days. I was more disappointed than a young lady living in a town, or a bustling neighborhood can possibly imagine. This visit, and the new acquaintance it promised, had furnished my day dream for many weeks.

"And how soon does he come?" I asked.

"Not till autumn. Not for two months, I dare say," he answered. "And I am very glad now, dear, that you never knew Mademoiselle Rheinfeldt."

"And why?" I asked, both mortified and curious.

"Because the poor young lady is dead," he replied. "I quite forgot I had not told you, but you were not in the room when I received the General's letter this evening."

I was very much shocked. General Spielsdorf had mentioned in his first letter, six or seven weeks before, that she was not so well as he would wish her, but there was nothing to suggest the remotest suspicion of danger.

"Here is the General's letter," he said, handing it to me. "I am afraid he is in great affliction; the letter appears to me to have been written very nearly in distraction."

We sat down on a rude bench, under a group of magnificent lime trees. The sun was setting with all its melancholy splendor behind the sylvan horizon, and the stream that flows beside our home, and passes under the steep old bridge I have mentioned, wound through many a group of noble trees, almost at our feet, reflecting in its current the fading crimson of the sky. General Spielsdorf's letter was so extraordinary, so vehement, and in some places so self-contradictory, that I read it twice over—the second time aloud to my father—and was still unable to account for it, except by supposing that grief had unsettled his mind.

It said "I have lost my darling daughter, for as such I loved her. During the last days of dear Bertha's illness I was not able to write to you. Before then I had no idea of her danger. I have lost her, and now learn *all*, too late. She died in the peace of innocence, and in the glorious hope of a blessed futurity. The fiend who betrayed our infatuated hospitality has done it all. I thought I was receiving into my house innocence, gaiety, a charming companion for my lost Bertha. Heavens! what a fool have I been! I thank God my child died without a suspicion of the cause of her sufferings. She is gone without so much as conjecturing the nature of her illness, and the accursed passion of the agent of all this misery. I devote my remaining days to tracking and extinguishing a monster. I am told I may hope to accomplish my righteous and merciful purpose. At present there is scarcely a gleam of light to guide me. I curse my conceited incredulity, my despicable affectation of superiority, my blindness, my obstinacy—all—too late. I cannot write or talk collectedly now. I am distracted. So soon as I shall have a little recovered, I mean to devote myself for a time to enquiry, which may possibly lead me as far as Vienna. Some time in the autumn, two months hence, or earlier if I live, I will see you—that is, if you permit me; I will then tell you all that I scarce dare put upon paper now. Farewell. Pray for me, dear friend."

In these terms ended this strange letter. Though I had never seen Bertha Rheinfeldt, my eyes filled with tears at the sudden intelligence; I was startled, as well as profoundly disappointed.

The sun had now set, and it was twilight by the time I had returned the General's letter to my father.

It was a soft clear evening, and we loitered, speculating upon the possible meanings of the violent and incoherent sentences which I had just been reading. We had nearly a mile to walk before reaching the road that passes the schloss in front, and by that time the moon was shining brilliantly. At the drawbridge we met Madame Perrodon and Mademoiselle De Lafontaine, who had come out, without their bonnets, to enjoy the exquisite moonlight.

We heard their voices gabbling in animated dialogue as we approached. We joined them at the drawbridge, and turned about to admire with them the beautiful scene.

The glade through which we had just walked lay before us. At our left the narrow road wound away under clumps of lordly trees, and was lost to sight amid the thickening forest. At the right the same road crosses the steep and picturesque bridge, near which stands a ruined tower which once guarded that pass; and beyond the bridge an abrupt eminence rises, covered with trees, and showing in the shadow, some grey ivy-clustered rocks.

Over the sward and low grounds, a thin film of mist was stealing like smoke, marking the distances with a transparent veil; and here and there we could see the river faintly flashing in the moonlight.

No softer, sweeter scene could be imagined. The news I had just heard made it melancholy; but nothing could disturb its character of profound serenity, and the enchanted glory and vagueness of the prospect.

My father, who enjoyed the picturesque, and I, stood looking in silence over the expanse beneath us. The two good governesses, standing a little way behind us, discoursed upon the scene, and were eloquent upon the moon.

Madame Perrodon was fat, middle-aged, and romantic, and talked and sighed poetically. Mademoiselle De Lafontaine—in right of her father who was a German, assumed to be psychological, metaphysical, and something of a mystic—now declared that when the moon shone with a light so intense it was well known that it indicated a special spiritual activity. The effect of the full moon in such a state of brilliancy was manifold. It acted on dreams, it acted on lunacy, it acted on nervous people, it had marvelous physical influences connected with life. Mademoiselle related that her cousin, who was mate of a merchant ship, having taken a nap on deck on such a night, lying on his back, with his face full in the light on the moon, had wakened, after a dream of an old woman clawing him by the cheek, with his features horribly drawn to one side; and his countenance had never quite recovered its equilibrium.

"The moon, this night," she said, "is full of odylic and magnetic influence—and see, when you look behind you at the front of the schloss how all its windows flash and twinkle with that silvery splendour, as if unseen hands had lighted up the rooms to receive fairy guests."

There are indolent states of the spirits in which, indisposed to talk ourselves, the talk of others is pleasant to our listless ears; and I gazed on, pleased with the tinkle of the ladies' conversation.

"I have got into one of my moping moods tonight," said my father, after a silence, and quoting Shakespeare, whom, by way of keeping up our English, he used to read aloud, he said:

"'In truth I know not why I am so sad:
It wearies me: you say it wearies you;
But how I got it—came by it.'

"I forget the rest. But I feel as if some great misfortune were hanging over us. I suppose the poor General's afflicted letter has had something to do with it."

At this moment the unwonted sound of carriage wheels and many hoofs upon the road, arrested our attention.

They seemed to be approaching from the high ground overlooking the bridge, and very soon the equipage emerged from that point. Two horsemen first crossed the bridge, then came a carriage drawn by four horses, and two men rode behind.

It seemed to be the traveling carriage of a person of rank; and we were all immediately absorbed in watching that very unusual spectacle. It became, in a few moments, greatly more interesting, for just as the carriage had passed the summit of the steep bridge, one of the leaders, taking fright, communicated his panic to the rest, and after a plunge or two, the whole team broke into a wild gallop together, and dashing between the horsemen who rode in front, came thundering along the road towards us with the speed of a hurricane.

The excitement of the scene was made more painful by the clear, long-drawn screams of a female voice from the carriage window.

We all advanced in curiosity and horror; my father in silence, the rest with various ejaculations of terror.

Our suspense did not last long. Just before you reach the castle drawbridge, on the route they were coming, there stands by the roadside a magnificent lime tree, on the other stands an ancient stone cross, at sight of which the horses, now going at a pace that was perfectly frightful, swerved so as to bring the wheel over the projecting roots of the tree.

I knew what was coming. I covered my eyes, unable to see it out, and turned my head away; at the same moment I heard a cry from my lady friends, who had gone on a little.

Curiosity opened my eyes, and I saw a scene of utter confusion. Two of the horses were on the ground, the carriage lay upon its side, with two wheels in the air; the men were busy removing the traces, and a lady, with a commanding air and figure had got out, and stood with clasped hands, raising the handkerchief that was in them every now and then to her eyes. Through the carriage door was now lifted a young lady, who appeared to be lifeless. My dear old father was already beside the elder lady, with his hat in his hand, evidently tendering his aid and the resources of his schloss. The lady did not appear to hear him, or to have eyes for anything but the slender girl who was being placed against the slope of the bank.

I approached; the young lady was apparently stunned, but she was certainly not dead. My father, who piqued himself on being something of a physician, had just had his fingers to her wrist and assured the lady, who declared herself her mother, that her pulse, though faint and irregular, was undoubtedly still distinguishable. The lady clasped her hands and looked upward, as if in a momentary transport of gratitude; but immediately she broke out again in that theatrical way which is, I believe, natural to some people.

She was what is called a fine looking woman for her time of life, and must have been handsome; she was tall, but not thin, and dressed in black velvet, and looked rather pale, but with a proud and commanding countenance, though now agitated strangely.

"Was ever being so born to calamity?" I heard her say, with clasped hands, as I came up. "Here am I, on a journey of life and death, in prosecuting which to lose an hour is possibly to lose all. My child will not have recovered sufficiently to resume her route for who can say how long. I must leave her: I cannot, dare not, delay. How far on, sir, can you tell, is the nearest village? I must leave her there; and shall not see my darling, or even hear of her till my return, three months hence."

I plucked my father by the coat, and whispered earnestly in his ear: "Oh! papa, pray ask her to let her stay with us—it would be so delightful. Do, pray."

"If Madame will entrust her child to the care of my daughter, and of her good gouvernante, Madame Perrodon, and permit her to remain as our guest, under my charge, until her return, it will confer a distinction and an obligation upon us, and we shall treat her with all the care and devotion which so sacred a trust deserves."

"I cannot do that, sir, it would be to task your kindness and chivalry too cruelly," said the lady, distractedly.

"It would, on the contrary, be to confer on us a very great kindness at the moment when we most need it. My daughter has just been disappointed by a cruel misfortune, in a visit from which she had long anticipated a great deal of happiness. If you confide this young lady to our care it will be her best consolation. The nearest village on your route is distant, and affords no such inn as you could think of placing your daughter at; you cannot allow her to continue her journey for any considerable distance without danger. If, as you say, you cannot suspend your journey, you must part with her tonight, and nowhere could you do so with more honest assurances of care and tenderness than here."

There was something in this lady's air and appearance so distinguished and even imposing, and in her manner so engaging, as to impress one, quite apart from the dignity of her equipage, with a conviction that she was a person of consequence.

By this time the carriage was replaced in its upright position, and the horses, quite tractable, in the traces again.

The lady threw on her daughter a glance which I fancied was not quite so affectionate as one might have anticipated from the beginning of the scene; then she beckoned slightly to my father, and withdrew two or three steps with him out of hearing; and talked to him with a fixed and stern countenance, not at all like that with which she had hitherto spoken.

I was filled with wonder that my father did not seem to perceive the change, and also unspeakably curious to learn what it could be that she was speaking, almost in his ear, with so much earnestness and rapidity.

Two or three minutes at most, I think, she remained thus employed, then she turned, and a few steps brought her to where her daughter lay, supported by Madame Perrodon. She kneeled beside her for a moment and whispered, as Madame supposed, a little benediction in her ear; then hastily kissing her, she stepped into her carriage, the door was closed, the footmen in stately liveries jumped up behind, the outriders spurred on, the postilions cracked their whips, the horses plunged and broke suddenly into a furious canter that threatened soon again to become a gallop, and the carriage whirled away, followed at the same rapid pace by the two horsemen in the rear.

CHAPTER III.

WE COMPARE NOTES

We followed the *cortège* with our eyes until it was swiftly lost to sight in the misty wood; and the very sound of the hoofs and the wheels died away in the silent night air.

Nothing remained to assure us that the adventure had not been an illusion of a moment but the young lady, who just at that moment opened her eyes. I could not see, for her face was turned from me, but she raised her head, evidently looking about her, and I heard a very sweet voice ask complainingly, "Where is mamma?"

Our good Madame Perrodon answered tenderly, and added some comfortable assurances.

I then heard her ask:

"Where am I? What is this place?" and after that she said, "I don't see the carriage; and Matska, where is she?"

Madame answered all her questions in so far as she understood
them; and gradually the young lady remembered how the mis-
adventure came about, and was glad to hear that no one in, or in
attendance on, the carriage was hurt; and on learning that her
mamma had left her here, till her return in about three months,
she wept.

I was going to add my consolations to those of Madame Perrodon when Mademoiselle De Lafontaine placed her hand upon
my arm, saying:

"Don't approach, one at a time is as much as she can at present
converse with; a very little excitement would possibly overpower
her now."

As soon as she is comfortably in bed, I thought, I will run up
to her room and see her.

My father in the meantime had sent a servant on horseback for
the physician, who lived about two leagues away; and a bedroom
was being prepared for the young lady's reception.

The stranger now rose, and leaning on Madame's arm, walked
slowly over the drawbridge and into the castle gate.

In the hall, servants waited to receive her, and she was conducted
forthwith to her room.

The room we usually sat in as our drawing-room is long, having
four windows, that looked over the moat and drawbridge, upon
the forest scene I have just described.

It is furnished in old carved oak, with large carved cabinets, and
the chairs are cushioned with crimson Utrecht velvet. The walls are
covered with tapestry, and surrounded with great gold frames, the

figures being as large as life, in ancient and very curious costume, and the subjects represented are hunting, hawking, and generally festive. It is not too stately to be extremely comfortable; and here we had our tea, for with his usual patriotic leanings he insisted that the national beverage should make its appearance regularly with our coffee and chocolate.

We sat here this night, and with candles lighted, were talking over the adventure of the evening.

Madame Perrodon and Mademoiselle De Lafontaine were both of our party. The young stranger had hardly lain down in her bed when she sank into a deep sleep; and those ladies had left her in the care of a servant.

"How do you like our guest?" I asked, as soon as Madame entered. "Tell me all about her?"

"I like her extremely," answered Madame, "she is, I almost think, the prettiest creature I ever saw; about your age, and so gentle and nice."

"She is absolutely beautiful," threw in Mademoiselle, who had peeped for a moment into the stranger's room.

"And such a sweet voice!" added Madame Perrodon.

"Did you remark a woman in the carriage, after it was set up again, who did not get out," inquired Mademoiselle, "but only looked from the window?"

"No, we had not seen her."

Then she described a hideous black woman, with a sort of colored turban on her head, and who was gazing all the time from the carriage window, nodding and grinning derisively towards the ladies, with gleaming eyes and large white eyeballs, and her teeth set as if in fury.

"Did you remark what an ill-looking pack of men the servants were?" asked Madame.

"Yes," said my father, who had just come in, "ugly, hang-dog looking fellows as ever I beheld in my life. I hope they mayn't rob the poor lady in the forest. They are clever rogues, however; they got everything to rights in a minute."

"I dare say they are worn out with too long traveling," said Madame.

"Besides looking wicked, their faces were so strangely lean, and dark, and sullen. I am very curious, I own; but I dare say the young lady will tell you all about it tomorrow, if she is sufficiently recovered."

"I don't think she will," said my father, with a mysterious smile, and a little nod of his head, as if he knew more about it than he cared to tell us.

This made us all the more inquisitive as to what had passed between him and the lady in the black velvet, in the brief but earnest interview that had immediately preceded her departure.

We were scarcely alone, when I entreated him to tell me. He did not need much pressing.

"There is no particular reason why I should not tell you. She expressed a reluctance to trouble us with the care of her daughter, saying she was in delicate health, and nervous, but not subject to any kind of seizure—she volunteered that—nor to any illusion; being, in fact, perfectly sane."

"How very odd to say all that!" I interpolated. "It was so unnecessary."

"At all events it *was* said," he laughed, "and as you wish to know all that passed, which was indeed very little, I tell you. She then said, 'I am making a long journey of *vital* importance—she emphasized the word—rapid and secret; I shall return for my child in three months; in the meantime, she will be silent as to who we are, whence we come, and whither we are traveling.' That is all she said. She spoke very pure French. When she said the word 'secret,' she paused for a few seconds, looking sternly, her eyes fixed on mine. I fancy she makes a great point of that. You saw how quickly she was gone. I hope I have not done a very foolish thing, in taking charge of the young lady."

For my part, I was delighted. I was longing to see and talk to her; and only waiting till the doctor should give me leave. You, who live in towns, can have no idea how great an event the introduction of a new friend is, in such a solitude as surrounded us.

The doctor did not arrive till nearly one o'clock; but I could no more have gone to my bed and slept, than I could have overtaken, on foot, the carriage in which the princess in black velvet had driven away.

When the physician came down to the drawing room, it was to report very favorably upon his patient. She was now sitting up, her pulse quite regular, apparently perfectly well. She had sustained no injury, and the little shock to her nerves had passed away quite harmlessly. There could be no harm certainly in my seeing her, if we both wished it; and, with this permission I sent, forthwith, to know whether she would allow me to visit her for a few minutes in her room.

The servant returned immediately to say that she desired nothing more.

You may be sure I was not long in availing myself of this permission.

Our visitor lay in one of the handsomest rooms in the schloss. It was, perhaps, a little stately. There was a somber piece of tapestry opposite the foot of the bed, representing Cleopatra with the asps to her bosom; and other solemn classic scenes were displayed, a little faded, upon the other walls. But there was gold carving, and rich and varied color enough in the other decorations of the room, to more than redeem the gloom of the old tapestry.

There were candles at the bedside. She was sitting up; her slender pretty figure enveloped in the soft silk dressing-gown, embroidered with flowers, and lined with thick quilted silk, which her mother had thrown over her feet as she lay upon the ground.

What was it that, as I reached the bedside and had just begun my little greeting, struck me dumb in a moment, and made me recoil a step or two from before her? I will tell you.

I saw the very face which had visited me in my childhood at night, which remained so fixed in my memory, and on which I had for so many years so often ruminated with horror, when no one suspected of what I was thinking.

It was pretty, even beautiful; and when I first beheld it, wore the same melancholy expression.

But this almost instantly lighted into a strange fixed smile of recognition.

There was a silence of fully a minute, and then at length *she* spoke; *I* could not.

"How wonderful!" she exclaimed. "Twelve years ago, I saw your face in a dream, and it has haunted me ever since."

"Wonderful indeed!" I repeated, overcoming with an effort the horror that had for a time suspended my utterances. "Twelve years ago, in vision or reality, *I* certainly saw you. I could not forget your face. It has remained before my eyes ever since."

Her smile had softened. Whatever I had fancied strange in it, was gone, and it and her dimpling cheeks were now delightfully pretty and intelligent.

I felt reassured, and continued more in the vein which hospitality indicated, to bid her welcome, and to tell her how much pleasure her accidental arrival had given us all, and especially what a happiness it was to me.

I took her hand as I spoke. I was a little shy, as lonely people are, but the situation made me eloquent, and even bold. She pressed my hand, she laid hers upon it, and her eyes glowed, as, looking hastily into mine, she smiled again, and blushed.

She answered my welcome very prettily. I sat down beside her, still wondering; and she said:

"I must tell you my vision about you; it is so very strange that you and I should have had, each of the other so vivid a dream, that each should have seen, I you and you me, looking as we do now, when of course we both were mere children. I was a child, about six years old, and I awoke from a confused and troubled dream, and found myself in a room, unlike my nursery, wainscoted clumsily in some dark wood, and with cupboards and bedsteads, and chairs, and benches placed about it. The beds were, I thought, all empty, and the room itself without anyone but myself in it; and I, after looking about me for some time, and admiring especially an iron candlestick with two branches, which I should certainly know again, crept under one of the beds to reach the window; but as I got from under the bed, I heard someone crying; and looking up, while I was still upon my knees, I saw *you*—most assuredly you—as I see you now; a beautiful young lady, with golden hair and large blue eyes, and lips—your lips—you as you are here. Your looks won me; I climbed on the bed and put my arms about you, and I think we both fell asleep. I was aroused by a scream; you were sitting up screaming. I was frightened, and slipped down upon the ground, and, it seemed to me, lost consciousness for a moment; and when I came to myself, I was again in my nursery at home. Your face I have never forgotten since. I could not be misled by mere resemblance. *You are* the lady whom I saw then."

It was now my turn to relate my corresponding vision, which I did, to the undisguised wonder of my new acquaintance.

"I don't know which should be most afraid of the other," she said, again smiling—"If you were less pretty I think I should be very much afraid of you, but being as you are, and you and I both so young, I feel only that I have made your acquaintance twelve years ago, and have already a right to your intimacy; at all events it does seem as if we were destined, from our earliest childhood, to be friends. I wonder whether you feel as strangely drawn towards me as I do to you; I have never had a friend—shall I find one now?" She sighed, and her fine dark eyes gazed passionately on me.

Now the truth is, I felt rather unaccountably towards the beautiful stranger. I did feel, as she said, "drawn towards her," but there was also something of repulsion. In this ambiguous feeling, however, the sense of attraction immensely prevailed. She interested and won me; she was so beautiful and so indescribably engaging.

I perceived now something of languor and exhaustion stealing over her, and hastened to bid her good night.

"The doctor thinks," I added, "that you ought to have a maid to sit up with you tonight; one of ours is waiting, and you will find her a very useful and quiet creature."

"How kind of you, but I could not sleep, I never could with an attendant in the room. I shan't require any assistance—and, shall I confess my weakness, I am haunted with a terror of robbers. Our house was robbed once, and two servants murdered, so I always lock my door. It has become a habit—and you look so kind I know you will forgive me. I see there is a key in the lock."

She held me close in her pretty arms for a moment and whispered in my ear, "Good night, darling, it is very hard to part with you, but good night; tomorrow, but not early, I shall see you again."

She sank back on the pillow with a sigh, and her fine eyes followed me with a fond and melancholy gaze, and she murmured again "Good night, dear friend."

Young people like, and even love, on impulse. I was flattered by the evident, though as yet undeserved, fondness she showed me. I liked the confidence with which she at once received me. She was determined that we should be very dear friends.

Next day came and we met again. I was delighted with my companion; that is to say, in many respects.

Her looks lost nothing in daylight—she was certainly the most beautiful creature I had ever seen, and the unpleasant remembrance of the face presented in my early dream, had lost the effect of the first unexpected recognition.

She confessed that she had experienced a similar shock on seeing me, and precisely the same faint antipathy that had mingled with my admiration of her. We now laughed together over our momentary horrors.

CHAPTER IV

HER HABITS—A SAUNTER

I told you that I was charmed with her in most particulars.

There were some that did not please me so well.

She was above the middle height of women. I shall begin by describing her. She was slender, and wonderfully graceful. Except that her movements were languid—*very* languid—indeed, there was nothing in her appearance to indicate an invalid. Her complexion was rich and brilliant; her features were small and beautifully formed; her eyes large, dark, and lustrous; her hair was quite wonderful, I never saw hair so magnificently thick and long when it was down about her shoulders; I have often placed my hands under it, and laughed with wonder at its weight. It was exquisitely fine and soft, and in color a rich very dark brown, with something of gold. I loved to let it down, tumbling with its own weight, as, in her room, she lay back in her chair talking in her sweet low voice, I used to fold and braid it, and spread it out and play with it. Heavens! If I had but known all!

I said there were particulars which did not please me. I have told you that her confidence won me the first night I saw her; but I found that she exercised with respect to herself, her mother, her history, everything in fact connected with her life, plans, and people, an ever wakeful reserve. I dare say I was unreasonable, perhaps I was wrong; I dare say I ought to have respected the solemn injunction laid upon my father by the stately lady in black velvet. But curiosity is a restless and unscrupulous passion, and no one girl can endure, with patience, that hers should be baffled by another. What harm could it do anyone to tell me what I so ardently desired to know? Had she no trust in my good sense or honor? Why would she not believe me when I assured her, so solemnly, that I would not divulge one syllable of what she told me to any mortal breathing.

There was a coldness, it seemed to me, beyond her years, in her smiling melancholy persistent refusal to afford me the least ray of light.

I cannot say we quarreled upon this point, for she would not quarrel upon any. It was, of course, very unfair of me to press her, very ill-bred, but I really could not help it; and I might just as well have let it alone.

What she did tell me amounted, in my unconscionable estimation—to nothing.

It was all summed up in three very vague disclosures:

First—Her name was Carmilla.

Second—Her family was very ancient and noble.

Third—Her home lay in the direction of the west.

She would not tell me the name of her family, nor their armorial bearings, nor the name of their estate, nor even that of the country they lived in.

You are not to suppose that I worried her incessantly on these subjects. I watched opportunity, and rather insinuated than urged my inquiries. Once or twice, indeed, I did attack her more directly. But no matter what my tactics, utter failure was invariably the result. Reproaches and caresses were all lost upon her. But I must add this, that her evasion was conducted with so pretty a melancholy and deprecation, with so many, and even passionate declarations of her liking for me, and trust in my honor, and with so many promises that I should at last know all, that I could not find it in my heart long to be offended with her.

She used to place her pretty arms about my neck, draw me to her, and laying her cheek to mine, murmur with her lips near my ear, "Dearest, your little heart is wounded; think me not cruel because I obey the irresistible law of my strength and weakness; if your dear heart is wounded, my wild heart bleeds with yours. In the rapture of my enormous humiliation I live in your warm life, and you shall die—die, sweetly die—into mine. I cannot help it; as I draw near to you, you, in your turn, will draw near to others, and learn the rapture of that cruelty, which yet is love; so, for a while, seek to know no more of me and mine, but trust me with all your loving spirit."

And when she had spoken such a rhapsody, she would press me more closely in her trembling embrace, and her lips in soft kisses gently glow upon my cheek.

Her agitations and her language were unintelligible to me.

From these foolish embraces, which were not of very frequent occurrence, I must allow, I used to wish to extricate myself; but my energies seemed to fail me. Her murmured words sounded like a lullaby in my ear, and soothed my resistance into a trance, from which I only seemed to recover myself when she withdrew her arms.

In these mysterious moods I did not like her. I experienced a strange tumultuous excitement that was pleasurable, ever and anon, mingled with a vague sense of fear and disgust. I had no distinct thoughts about her while such scenes lasted, but I was conscious of a love growing into adoration, and also of abhorrence. This I know is paradox, but I can make no other attempt to explain the feeling.

I now write, after an interval of more than ten years, with a trembling hand, with a confused and horrible recollection of certain occurrences and situations, in the ordeal through which I was unconsciously passing; though with a vivid and very sharp remembrance of the main current of my story. But, I suspect, in all lives there are certain emotional scenes, those in which our passions have been most wildly and terribly roused, that are of all others the most vaguely and dimly remembered.

Sometimes after an hour of apathy, my strange and beautiful companion would take my hand and hold it with a fond pressure, renewed again and again; blushing softly, gazing in my face with languid and burning eyes, and breathing so fast that her dress rose and fell with the tumultuous respiration. It was like the ardor of a lover; it embarrassed me; it was hateful and yet over-powering; and with gloating eyes she drew me to her, and her hot lips traveled along my cheek in kisses; and she would whisper, almost in sobs, "You are mine, you *shall* be mine, you and I are one for ever." Then she had thrown herself back in her chair, with her small hands over her eyes, leaving me trembling.

"Are we related," I used to ask; "what can you mean by all this? I remind you perhaps of someone whom you love; but you must not, I hate it; I don't know you—I don't know myself when you look so and talk so."

She used to sigh at my vehemence, then turn away and drop my hand.

Respecting these very extraordinary manifestations I strove in vain to form any satisfactory theory—I could not refer them to affectation or trick. It was unmistakably the momentary breaking out of suppressed instinct and emotion. Was she, notwithstanding her mother's volunteered denial, subject to brief visitations of insanity; or was there here a disguise and a romance? I had read in old storybooks of such things. What if a boyish lover had found his way into the house, and sought to prosecute his suit in masquerade, with the assistance of a clever old adventuress. But there were many things against this hypothesis, highly interesting as it was to my vanity.

I could boast of no little attentions such as masculine gallantry delights to offer. Between these passionate moments there were long intervals of commonplace, of gaiety, of brooding melancholy, during which, except that I detected her eyes so full of melancholy fire, following me, at times I might have been as nothing to her. Except in these brief periods of mysterious excitement her ways were girlish; and there was always a languor about her, quite incompatible with a masculine system in a state of health.

In some respects her habits were odd. Perhaps not so singular in the opinion of a town lady like you, as they appeared to us rustic people. She used to come down very late, generally not till one o'clock, she would then take a cup of chocolate, but eat nothing; we then went out for a walk, which was a mere saunter, and she seemed, almost immediately, exhausted, and either returned to the schloss or sat on one of the benches that were placed, here and there, among the trees. This was a bodily languor in which her mind did not sympathize. She was always an animated talker, and very intelligent.

She sometimes alluded for a moment to her own home, or mentioned an adventure or situation, or an early recollection, which indicated a people of strange manners, and described customs of which we knew nothing. I gathered from these chance hints that her native country was much more remote than I had at first fancied.

As we sat thus one afternoon under the trees a funeral passed us by. It was that of a pretty young girl, whom I had often seen, the daughter of one of the rangers of the forest. The poor man was walking behind the coffin of his darling; she was his only child, and he looked quite heartbroken. Peasants walking two-and-two came behind, they were singing a funeral hymn.

I rose to mark my respect as they passed, and joined in the hymn they were very sweetly singing.

My companion shook me a little roughly, and I turned surprised. She said brusquely, "Don't you perceive how discordant that is?"

"I think it very sweet, on the contrary," I answered, vexed at the interruption, and very uncomfortable, lest the people who composed the little procession should observe and resent what was passing.

I resumed, therefore, instantly, and was again interrupted. "You pierce my ears," said Carmilla, almost angrily, and stopping her ears with her tiny fingers. "Besides, how can you tell that your religion and mine are the same; your forms wound me, and I hate funerals. What a fuss! Why *you* must die—*everyone* must die; and all are happier when they do. Come home."

"My father has gone on with the clergyman to the churchyard. I thought you knew she was to be buried today."

"*She?* I don't trouble my head about peasants. I don't know who she is," answered Carmilla, with a flash from her fine eyes.

"She is the poor girl who fancied she saw a ghost a fortnight ago, and has been dying ever since, till yesterday, when she expired."

"Tell me nothing about ghosts. I shan't sleep tonight if you do."

"I hope there is no plague or fever coming; all this looks very like it," I continued. "The swineherd's young wife died only a week ago, and she thought something seized her by the throat as she lay in her bed, and nearly strangled her. Papa says such horrible fancies do accompany some forms of fever. She was quite well the day before. She sank afterwards, and died before a week."

"Well, *her* funeral is over, I hope, and *her* hymn sung; and our ears shan't be tortured with that discord and jargon. It has made me nervous. Sit down here, beside me; sit close; hold my hand; press it hard—hard—harder."

We had moved a little back, and had come to another seat.

She sat down. Her face underwent a change that alarmed and even terrified me for a moment. It darkened, and became horribly livid; her teeth and hands were clenched, and she frowned and compressed her lips, while she stared down upon the ground at her feet, and trembled all over with a continued shudder as irrepressible as ague. All her energies seemed strained to suppress a fit, with which she was then breathlessly tugging; and at length a low convulsive cry of suffering broke from her, and gradually the hysteria subsided. "There! That comes of strangling people with hymns!" she said at last. "Hold me, hold me still. It is passing away."

And so gradually it did; and perhaps to dissipate the somber impression which the spectacle had left upon me, she became unusually animated and chatty; and so we got home.

This was the first time I had seen her exhibit any definable symptoms of that delicacy of health which her mother had spoken of. It was the first time, also, I had seen her exhibit anything like temper.

Both passed away like a summer cloud; and never but once afterwards did I witness on her part a momentary sign of anger. I will tell you how it happened.

She and I were looking out of one of the long drawing room windows, when there entered the courtyard, over the drawbridge, a figure of a wanderer whom I knew very well. He used to visit the schloss generally twice a year.

It was the figure of a hunchback, with the sharp lean features that generally accompany deformity. He wore a pointed black beard, and he was smiling from ear to ear, showing his white fangs. He was dressed in buff, black, and scarlet, and crossed with more straps and belts than I could count, from which hung all manner of things. Behind, he carried a magic lantern, and two boxes, which I well knew, in one of which was a salamander, and in the other a mandrake. These monsters used to make my father laugh. They were compounded of parts of monkeys, parrots, squirrels, fish, and hedgehogs, dried and stitched together with great neatness and startling effect. He had a fiddle, a box of conjuring apparatus, a pair of foils and masks attached to his belt, several other mysterious cases dangling about him, and a black staff with copper ferrules in his hand. His companion was a rough spare dog, that followed at his heels, but stopped short, suspiciously at the drawbridge, and in a little while began to howl dismally.

In the meantime, the mountebank, standing in the midst of the courtyard, raised his grotesque hat, and made us a very ceremonious bow, paying his compliments very volubly in execrable French, and German not much better. Then, disengaging his fiddle, he began to scrape a lively air to which he sang with a merry discord, dancing with ludicrous airs and activity, that made me laugh, in spite of the dog's howling.

Then he advanced to the window with many smiles and salutations, and his hat in his left hand, his fiddle under his arm, and with a fluency that never took breath, he gabbled a long advertisement of all his accomplishments, and the resources of the various arts which he placed at our service, and the curiosities and entertainments which it was in his power, at our bidding, to display.

"Will your ladyships be pleased to buy an amulet against the oupire, which is going like the wolf, I hear, through these woods," he said dropping his hat on the pavement. "They are dying of it right and left and here is a charm that never fails; only pinned to the pillow, and you may laugh in his face."

These charms consisted of oblong slips of vellum, with cabalistic ciphers and diagrams upon them.

Carmilla instantly purchased one, and so did I.

He was looking up, and we were smiling down upon him, amused; at least, I can answer for myself. His piercing black eye, as he looked up in our faces, seemed to detect something that fixed for a moment his curiosity.

In an instant he unrolled a leather case, full of all manner of odd little steel instruments.

"See here, my lady," he said, displaying it, and addressing me, "I profess, among other things less useful, the art of dentistry. Plague take the dog!" he interpolated. "Silence, beast! He howls so that your ladyships can scarcely hear a word. Your noble friend, the young lady at your right, has the sharpest tooth,—long, thin, pointed, like an awl, like a needle; ha, ha! With my sharp and long sight, as I look up, I have seen it distinctly; now if it happens to hurt the young lady, and I think it must, here am I, here are my file, my punch, my nippers; I will make it round and blunt, if her ladyship pleases; no longer the tooth of a fish, but of a beautiful young lady as she is. Hey? Is the young lady displeased? Have I been too bold? Have I offended her?"

The young lady, indeed, looked very angry as she drew back from the window.

"How dares that mountebank insult us so? Where is your father? I shall demand redress from him. My father would have had the wretch tied up to the pump, and flogged with a cart whip, and burnt to the bones with the castle brand!"

She retired from the window a step or two, and sat down, and had hardly lost sight of the offender, when her wrath subsided as suddenly as it had risen, and she gradually recovered her usual tone, and seemed to forget the little hunchback and his follies.

My father was out of spirits that evening. On coming in he told us that there had been another case very similar to the two fatal ones which had lately occurred. The sister of a young peasant on his estate, only a mile away, was very ill, had been, as she described it, attacked very nearly in the same way, and was now slowly but steadily sinking.

"All this," said my father, "is strictly referable to natural causes. These poor people infect one another with their superstitions, and so repeat in imagination the images of terror that have infested their neighbors."

"But that very circumstance frightens one horribly," said Carmilla.

"How so?" inquired my father.

"I am so afraid of fancying I see such things; I think it would be as bad as reality."

"We are in God's hands: nothing can happen without His permission, and all will end well for those who love Him. He is our faithful creator; He has made us all, and will take care of us."

"Creator! *Nature!*" said the young lady in answer to my gentle father. "And this disease that invades the country is natural. Nature. All things proceed from Nature—don't they? All things in the heaven, in the earth, and under the earth, act and live as Nature ordains? I think so."

"The doctor said he would come here today," said my father, after a silence. "I want to know what he thinks about it, and what he thinks we had better do."

"Doctors never did me any good," said Carmilla.

"Then you have been ill?" I asked.

"More ill than ever you were," she answered.

"Long ago?"

"Yes, a long time. I suffered from this very illness; but I forget all but my pain and weakness, and they were not so bad as are suffered in other diseases."

"You were very young then?"

"I dare say, let us talk no more of it. You would not wound a friend?" She looked languidly in my eyes, and passed her arm round my waist lovingly, and led me out of the room. My father was busy over some papers near the window.

"Why does your papa like to frighten us?" said the pretty girl, with a sigh and a little shudder.

"He doesn't, dear Carmilla, it is the very furthest thing from his mind."

"Are you afraid, dearest?"

"I should be very much if I fancied there was any real danger of my being attacked as those poor people were."

"You are afraid to die?"

"Yes, every one is."

"But to die as lovers may—to die together, so that they may live together. Girls are caterpillars while they live in the world, to be finally butterflies when the summer comes; but in the meantime there are grubs and larvae, don't you see—each with their peculiar propensities, necessities and structure. So says Monsieur Buffon, in his big book, in the next room."

Later in the day the doctor came, and was closeted with papa for some time.

He was a skilful man, of sixty and upwards, he wore powder, and shaved his pale face as smooth as a pumpkin. He and papa emerged from the room together, and I heard papa laugh, and say as they came out:

"Well, I do wonder at a wise man like you. What do you say to hippogriffs and dragons?"

The doctor was smiling, and made answer, shaking his head—

"Nevertheless life and death are mysterious states, and we know little of the resources of either."

And so they walked on, and I heard no more. I did not then know what the doctor had been broaching, but I think I guess it now.

CHAPTER V.

A WONDERFUL LIKENESS

This evening there arrived from Gratz the grave, dark-faced son of the picture cleaner, with a horse and cart laden with two large packing cases, having many pictures in each. It was a journey of ten leagues, and whenever a messenger arrived at the schloss from our little capital of Gratz, we used to crowd about him in the hall, to hear the news.

This arrival created in our secluded quarters quite a sensation. The cases remained in the hall, and the messenger was taken charge of by the servants till he had eaten his supper. Then with assistants, and armed with hammer, ripping chisel, and turn-screw, he met us in the hall, where we had assembled to witness the unpacking of the cases.

Carmilla sat looking listlessly on, while one after the other the old pictures, nearly all portraits, which had undergone the process of renovation, were brought to light. My mother was of an old Hungarian family, and most of these pictures, which were about to be restored to their places, had come to us through her.

My father had a list in his hand, from which he read, as the artist rummaged out the corresponding numbers. I don't know that the pictures were very good, but they were, undoubtedly, very old, and some of them very curious also. They had, for the most part, the merit of being now seen by me, I may say, for the first time; for the smoke and dust of time had all but obliterated them.

"There is a picture that I have not seen yet," said my father. "In one corner, at the top of it, is the name, as well as I could read, 'Marcia Karnstein,' and the date '1698'; and I am curious to see how it has turned out."

I remembered it; it was a small picture, about a foot and a half high, and nearly square, without a frame; but it was so blackened by age that I could not make it out.

The artist now produced it, with evident pride. It was quite beautiful; it was startling; it seemed to live. It was the effigy of Carmilla!

"Carmilla, dear, here is an absolute miracle. Here you are, living, smiling, ready to speak, in this picture. Isn't it beautiful, Papa? And see, even the little mole on her throat."

My father laughed, and said "Certainly it is a wonderful likeness," but he looked away, and to my surprise seemed but little struck by it, and went on talking to the picture cleaner, who was also something of an artist, and discoursed with intelligence about the portraits or other works, which his art had just brought into light and color, while *I* was more and more lost in wonder the more I looked at the picture.

"Will you let me hang this picture in my room, papa?" I asked.

"Certainly, dear," said he, smiling, "I'm very glad you think it so like. It must be prettier even than I thought it, if it is."

The young lady did not acknowledge this pretty speech, did not seem to hear it. She was leaning back in her seat, her fine eyes under their long lashes gazing on me in contemplation, and she smiled in a kind of rapture.

"And now you can read quite plainly the name that is written in the corner. It is not Marcia; it looks as if it was done in gold. The name is Mircalla, Countess Karnstein, and this is a little coronet over and underneath A.D. 1698. I am descended from the Karnsteins; that is, mamma was."

"Ah!" said the lady, languidly, "so am I, I think, a very long descent, very ancient. Are there any Karnsteins living now?"

"None who bear the name, I believe. The family were ruined, I believe, in some civil wars, long ago, but the ruins of the castle are only about three miles away."

"How interesting!" she said, languidly. "But see what beautiful moonlight!" She glanced through the hall door, which stood a little open. "Suppose you take a little ramble round the court, and look down at the road and river."

"It is so like the night you came to us," I said.

She sighed; smiling.

She rose, and each with her arm about the other's waist, we walked out upon the pavement.

In silence, slowly we walked down to the drawbridge, where the beautiful landscape opened before us.

"And so you were thinking of the night I came here?" she almost whispered. "Are you glad I came?"

"Delighted, dear Carmilla," I answered.

"And you asked for the picture you think like me, to hang in your room," she murmured with a sigh, as she drew her arm closer about my waist, and let her pretty head sink upon my shoulder.

"How romantic you are, Carmilla," I said. "Whenever you tell me your story, it will be made up chiefly of some one great romance."

She kissed me silently.

"I am sure, Carmilla, you have been in love; that there is, at this moment, an affair of the heart going on."

"I have been in love with no one, and never shall," she whispered, "unless it should be with you."

How beautiful she looked in the moonlight!

Shy and strange was the look with which she quickly hid her face in my neck and hair, with tumultuous sighs, that seemed almost to sob, and pressed in mine a hand that trembled.

Her soft cheek was glowing against mine. "Darling, darling," she murmured, "I live in you; and you would die for me, I love you so."

I started from her.

She was gazing on me with eyes from which all fire, all meaning had flown, and a face colourless and apathetic.

"Is there a chill in the air, dear?" she said drowsily. "I almost shiver; have I been dreaming? Let us come in. Come, come; come in."

"You look ill, Carmilla; a little faint. You certainly must take some wine," I said.

"Yes. I will. I'm better now. I shall be quite well in a few minutes. Yes, do give me a little wine," answered Carmilla, as we approached the door. "Let us look again for a moment; it is the last time, perhaps, I shall see the moonlight with you."

"How do you feel now, dear Carmilla? Are you really better?" I asked.

I was beginning to take alarm, lest she should have been stricken with the strange epidemic that they said had invaded the country about us.

"Papa would be grieved beyond measure," I added, "if he thought you were ever so little ill, without immediately letting us know. We have a very skilful doctor near us, the physician who was with papa today."

"I'm sure he is. I know how kind you all are; but, dear child, I am quite well again. There is nothing ever wrong with me, but a little weakness. People say I am languid; I am incapable of exertion; I can scarcely walk as far as a child of three years old; and every now and then the little strength I have falters, and I become as you have just seen me. But after all I am very easily set up again; in a moment I am perfectly myself. See how I have recovered."

So, indeed, she had; and she and I talked a great deal, and very animated she was; and the remainder of that evening passed without any recurrence of what I called her infatuations. I mean her crazy talk and looks, which embarrassed, and even frightened me.

But there occurred that night an event which gave my thoughts quite a new turn, and seemed to startle even Carmilla's languid nature into momentary energy.

CHAPTER VI.

A VERY STRANGE AGONY

When we got into the drawing room, and had sat down to our coffee and chocolate, although Carmilla did not take any, she seemed quite herself again, and Madame, and Mademoiselle De Lafontaine, joined us, and made a little card party, in the course of which papa came in for what he called his "dish of tea."

When the game was over he sat down beside Carmilla on the sofa, and asked her, a little anxiously, whether she had heard from her mother since her arrival.

She answered "No."

He then asked whether she knew where a letter would reach her at present.

"I cannot tell," she answered ambiguously, "but I have been thinking of leaving you; you have been already too hospitable and too kind to me. I have given you an infinity of trouble, and I should wish to take a carriage tomorrow, and post in pursuit of her; I know where I shall ultimately find her, although I dare not yet tell you."

"But you must not dream of any such thing," exclaimed my father, to my great relief. "We can't afford to lose you so, and I won't consent to your leaving us, except under the care of your mother, who was so good as to consent to your remaining with us till she should herself return. I should be quite happy if I knew that you heard from her: but this evening the accounts of the progress of the mysterious disease that has invaded our neighborhood, grow even more alarming; and my beautiful guest, I do feel the responsibility, unaided by advice from your mother, very much. But I shall do my best; and one thing is certain, that you must not think of leaving us without her distinct direction to that effect. We should suffer too much in parting from you to consent to it easily."

"Thank you, sir, a thousand times for your hospitality," she answered, smiling bashfully. "You have all been too kind to me; I have seldom been so happy in all my life before, as in your beautiful chateau, under your care, and in the society of your dear daughter."

So he gallantly, in his old-fashioned way, kissed her hand, smiling and pleased at her little speech.

I accompanied Carmilla as usual to her room, and sat and chatted with her while she was preparing for bed.

"Do you think," I said at length, "that you will ever confide fully in me?"

She turned round smiling, but made no answer, only continued to smile on me.

"You won't answer that?" I said. "You can't answer pleasantly; I ought not to have asked you."

"You were quite right to ask me that, or anything. You do not know how dear you are to me, or you could not think any confidence too great to look for. But I am under vows, no nun half so awfully, and I dare not tell my story yet, even to you. The time is very near when you shall know everything. You will think me cruel, very selfish, but love is always selfish; the more ardent the more selfish. How jealous I am you cannot know. You must come with me, loving me, to death; or else hate me and still come with me. and *hating* me through death and after. There is no such word as indifference in my apathetic nature."

"Now, Carmilla, you are going to talk your wild nonsense again," I said hastily.

"Not I, silly little fool as I am, and full of whims and fancies; for your sake I'll talk like a sage. Were you ever at a ball?"

"No; how you do run on. What is it like? How charming it must be."

"I almost forget, it is years ago."

I laughed.

"You are not so old. Your first ball can hardly be forgotten yet."

"I remember everything about it—with an effort. I see it all, as divers see what is going on above them, through a medium, dense, rippling, but transparent. There occurred that night what has confused the picture, and made its colours faint. I was all but assassinated in my bed, wounded *here*," she touched her breast, "and never was the same since."

"Were you near dying?"

"Yes, very—a cruel love—strange love, that would have taken my life. Love will have its sacrifices. No sacrifice without blood. Let us go to sleep now; I feel so lazy. How can I get up just now and lock my door?"

She was lying with her tiny hands buried in her rich wavy hair, under her cheek, her little head upon the pillow, and her glittering eyes followed me wherever I moved, with a kind of shy smile that I could not decipher.

I bid her good night, and crept from the room with an uncomfortable sensation.

I often wondered whether our pretty guest ever said her prayers. I certainly had never seen her upon her knees. In the morning she never came down until long after our family prayers were over, and at night she never left the drawing room to attend our brief evening prayers in the hall.

If it had not been that it had casually come out in one of our careless talks that she had been baptised, I should have doubted her being a Christian. Religion was a subject on which I had never heard her speak a word. If I had known the world better, this particular neglect or antipathy would not have so much surprised me.

The precautions of nervous people are infectious, and persons of a like temperament are pretty sure, after a time, to imitate them. I had adopted Carmilla's habit of locking her bedroom door, having taken into my head all her whimsical alarms about midnight invaders and prowling assassins. I had also adopted her precaution of making a brief search through her room, to satisfy herself that no lurking assassin or robber was "ensconced."

These wise measures taken, I got into my bed and fell asleep. A light was burning in my room. This was an old habit, of very early date, and which nothing could have tempted me to dispense with.

Thus fortified I might take my rest in peace. But dreams come through stone walls, light up dark rooms, or darken light ones, and their persons make their exits and their entrances as they please, and laugh at locksmiths.

I had a dream that night that was the beginning of a very strange agony.

I cannot call it a nightmare, for I was quite conscious of being asleep. But I was equally conscious of being in my room, and lying in bed, precisely as I actually was. I saw, or fancied I saw, the room and its furniture just as I had seen it last, except that it was very dark, and I saw something moving round the foot of the bed, which at first I could not accurately distinguish. But I soon saw that it was a sooty-black animal that resembled a monstrous cat. It appeared to me about four or five feet long for it measured fully the length of the hearthrug as it passed over it; and it continued to-ing and fro-ing with the lithe, sinister restlessness of a beast in a cage. I could not cry out, although as you may suppose, I was terrified. Its pace was growing faster, and the room rapidly darker and darker, and at length so dark that I could no longer see anything of it but its eyes. I felt it spring lightly on the bed. The two broad eyes approached my face, and suddenly I felt a stinging pain as if two large needles darted, an inch or two apart, deep into my breast. I waked with a scream. The room was lighted by the candle that burnt there all through the night, and I saw a female figure standing at the foot of the bed, a little at the right side. It was in a dark loose dress, and its hair was down and covered its shoulders. A block of stone could not have been more still. There was not the slightest stir of respiration. As I stared at it, the figure appeared to have changed its place, and was now nearer the door; then, close to it, the door opened, and it passed out.

I was now relieved, and able to breathe and move. My first thought was that Carmilla had been playing me a trick, and that I had forgotten to secure my door. I hastened to it, and found it locked as usual on the inside. I was afraid to open it—I was horrified. I sprang into my bed and covered my head up in the bedclothes, and lay there more dead than alive till morning.

CHAPTER VII.

DESCENDING

It would be vain my attempting to tell you the horror with which, even now, I recall the occurrence of that night. It was no such transitory terror as a dream leaves behind it. It seemed to deepen by time, and communicated itself to the room and the very furniture that had encompassed the apparition.

I could not bear next day to be alone for a moment. I should have told papa, but for two opposite reasons. At one time I thought he would laugh at my story, and I could not bear its being treated as a jest; and at another, I thought he might fancy that I had been attacked by the mysterious complaint which had invaded our neighborhood. I had myself no misgiving of the kind, and as he had been rather an invalid for some time, I was afraid of alarming him.

I was comfortable enough with my good-natured companions, Madame Perrodon, and the vivacious Mademoiselle Lafontaine.

They both perceived that I was out of spirits and nervous, and at length I told them what lay so heavy at my heart.

Mademoiselle laughed, but I fancied that Madame Perrodon looked anxious.

"By-the-by," said Mademoiselle, laughing, "the long lime tree walk, behind Carmilla's bedroom window, is haunted!"

"Nonsense!" exclaimed Madame, who probably thought the theme rather inopportune, "and who tells that story, my dear?"

"Martin says that he came up twice, when the old yard gate was being repaired, before sunrise, and twice saw the same female figure walking down the lime tree avenue."

"So he well might, as long as there are cows to milk in the river fields," said Madame.

"I daresay; but Martin chooses to be frightened, and never did I see fool *more* frightened."

"You must not say a word about it to Carmilla, because she can see down that walk from her room window," I interposed, "and she is, if possible, a greater coward than I."

Carmilla came down rather later than usual that day.

"I was so frightened last night," she said, so soon as were together, "and I am sure I should have seen something dreadful if it had not been for that charm I bought from the poor little hunchback whom I called such hard names. I had a dream of something black coming round my bed, and I awoke in a perfect horror, and I really thought, for some seconds, I saw a dark figure near the chimneypiece, but I felt under my pillow for my charm, and the moment my fingers touched it, the figure disappeared, and I felt quite certain, only that I had it by me, that something frightful would have made its appearance, and, perhaps, throttled me, as it did those poor people we heard of.

"Well, listen to me," I began, and recounted my adventure, at the recital of which she appeared horrified.

"And had you the charm near you?" she asked, earnestly.

"No, I had dropped it into a china vase in the drawing room, but I shall certainly take it with me tonight, as you have so much faith in it."

At this distance of time I cannot tell you, or even understand, how I overcame my horror so effectually as to lie alone in my room that night. I remember distinctly that I pinned the charm to my pillow. I fell asleep almost immediately, and slept even more soundly than usual all night.

Next night I passed as well. My sleep was delightfully deep and dreamless. But I wakened with a sense of lassitude and melancholy, which, however, did not exceed a degree that was almost luxurious.

"Well, I told you so," said Carmilla, when I described my quiet sleep, "I had such delightful sleep myself last night; I pinned the charm to the breast of my nightdress. It was too far away the night before. I am quite sure it was all fancy, except the dreams. I used to think that evil spirits made dreams, but our doctor told me it is no such thing. Only a fever passing by, or some other malady, as they often do, he said, knocks at the door, and not being able to get in, passes on, with that alarm."

"And what do you think the charm is?" said I.

"It has been fumigated or immersed in some drug, and is an antidote against the malaria," she answered.

"Then it acts only on the body?"

"Certainly; you don't suppose that evil spirits are frightened by bits of ribbon, or the perfumes of a druggist's shop? No, these complaints, wandering in the air, begin by trying the nerves, and so infect the brain, but before they can seize upon you, the antidote repels them. That I am sure is what the charm has done for us. It is nothing magical, it is simply natural.

I should have been happier if I could have quite agreed with Carmilla, but I did my best, and the impression was a little losing its force.

For some nights I slept profoundly; but still every morning I felt the same lassitude, and a languor weighed upon me all day. I felt myself a changed girl. A strange melancholy was stealing over me, a melancholy that I would not have interrupted. Dim thoughts of death began to open, and an idea that I was slowly sinking took gentle, and, somehow, not unwelcome, possession of me. If it was sad, the tone of mind which this induced was also sweet.

Whatever it might be, my soul acquiesced in it.

I would not admit that I was ill, I would not consent to tell my papa, or to have the doctor sent for.

Carmilla became more devoted to me than ever, and her strange paroxysms of languid adoration more frequent. She used to gloat on me with increasing ardor the more my strength and spirits waned. This always shocked me like a momentary glare of insanity.

Without knowing it, I was now in a pretty advanced stage of the strangest illness under which mortal ever suffered. There was an unaccountable fascination in its earlier symptoms that more than reconciled me to the incapacitating effect of that stage of the malady. This fascination increased for a time, until it reached a certain point, when gradually a sense of the horrible mingled itself with it, deepening, as you shall hear, until it discolored and perverted the whole state of my life.

The first change I experienced was rather agreeable. It was very near the turning point from which began the descent of Avernus.

Certain vague and strange sensations visited me in my sleep. The prevailing one was of that pleasant, peculiar cold thrill which we feel in bathing, when we move against the current of a river. This was soon accompanied by dreams that seemed interminable, and were so vague that I could never recollect their scenery and persons, or any one connected portion of their action. But they left an awful impression, and a sense of exhaustion, as if I had passed through a long period of great mental exertion and danger. After all these dreams there remained on waking a remembrance of having been in a place very nearly dark, and of having spoken to people whom I could not see; and especially of one clear voice, of a female's, very deep, that spoke as if at a distance, slowly, and producing always the same sensation of indescribable solemnity and fear. Sometimes there came a sensation as if a hand was drawn softly along my cheek and neck. Sometimes it was as if warm lips kissed me, and longer and longer and more lovingly as they reached my throat, but there the caress fixed itself. My heart beat faster, my breathing rose and fell rapidly and full drawn; a sobbing, that rose into a sense of strangulation, supervened, and turned into a dreadful convulsion, in which my senses left me and I became unconscious.

It was now three weeks since the commencement of this unaccountable state. My sufferings had, during the last week, told upon my appearance. I had grown pale, my eyes were dilated and darkened underneath, and the languor which I had long felt began to display itself in my countenance.

My father asked me often whether I was ill; but, with an obstinacy which now seems to me unaccountable, I persisted in assuring him that I was quite well.

In a sense this was true. I had no pain, I could complain of no bodily derangement. My complaint seemed to be one of the imagination, or the nerves, and, horrible as my sufferings were, I kept them, with a morbid reserve, very nearly to myself.

It could not be that terrible complaint which the peasants called the oupire, for I had now been suffering for three weeks, and they were seldom ill for much more than three days, when death put an end to their miseries.

Carmilla complained of dreams and feverish sensations, but by no means of so alarming a kind as mine. I say that mine were extremely alarming. Had I been capable of comprehending my condition, I would have invoked aid and advice on my knees. The narcotic of an unsuspected influence was acting upon me, and my perceptions were benumbed.

I am going to tell you now of a dream that led immediately to an odd discovery.

One night, instead of the voice I was accustomed to hear in the dark, I heard one, sweet and tender, and at the same time terrible, which said, "Your mother warns you to beware of the assassin." At the same time a light unexpectedly sprang up, and I saw Carmilla, standing, near the foot of my bed, in her white nightdress, bathed, from her chin to her feet, in one great stain of blood.

I wakened with a shriek, possessed with the one idea that Carmilla was being murdered. I remember springing from my bed, and my next recollection is that of standing on the lobby, crying for help.

Madame and Mademoiselle came scurrying out of their rooms in alarm; a lamp burned always on the lobby, and seeing me, they soon learned the cause of my terror.

I insisted on our knocking at Carmilla's door. Our knocking was unanswered. It soon became a pounding and an uproar. We shrieked her name, but all was vain.

We all grew frightened, for the door was locked. We hurried back, in panic, to my room. There we rang the bell long and furiously. If my father's room had been at that side of the house, we would have called him up at once to our aid. But, alas! he was quite out of hearing, and to reach him involved an excursion for which we none of us had courage.

Servants, however, soon came running up the stairs; I had got on my dressing gown and slippers meanwhile, and my companions were already similarly furnished. Recognizing the voices of the servants on the lobby, we sallied out together; and having renewed, as fruitlessly, our summons at Carmilla's door, I ordered the men to force the lock. They did so, and we stood, holding our lights aloft, in the doorway, and so stared into the room.

We called her by name; but there was still no reply. We looked round the room. Everything was undisturbed. It was exactly in the state in which I left it on bidding her good night. But Carmilla was gone.

CHAPTER VIII.

SEARCH

At sight of the room, perfectly undisturbed except for our violent entrance, we began to cool a little, and soon recovered our senses sufficiently to dismiss the men. It had struck Mademoiselle that possibly Carmilla had been wakened by the uproar at her door, and in her first panic had jumped from her bed, and hid herself in a press, or behind a curtain, from which she could not, of course, emerge until the majordomo and his myrmidons had withdrawn. We now recommenced our search, and began to call her name again.

It was all to no purpose. Our perplexity and agitation increased. We examined the windows, but they were secured. I implored of Carmilla, if she had concealed herself, to play this cruel trick no longer—to come out and to end our anxieties. It was all useless. I was by this time convinced that she was not in the room, nor in the dressing room, the door of which was still locked on this side. She could not have passed it. I was utterly puzzled. Had Carmilla discovered one of those secret passages which the old housekeeper said were known to exist in the schloss, although the tradition of their exact situation had been lost? A little time would, no doubt, explain all—utterly perplexed as, for the present, we were.

It was past four o'clock, and I preferred passing the remaining hours of darkness in Madame's room. Daylight brought no solution of the difficulty.

The whole household, with my father at its head, was in a state of agitation next morning. Every part of the chateau was searched. The grounds were explored. Not a trace of the missing lady could be discovered. The stream was about to be dragged; my father was in distraction; what a tale to have to tell the poor girl's mother on her return. I, too, was almost beside myself, though my grief was quite of a different kind.

The morning was passed in alarm and excitement. It was now one o'clock, and still no tidings. I ran up to Carmilla's room, and found her standing at her dressing table. I was astounded. I could not believe my eyes. She beckoned me to her with her pretty finger, in silence. Her face expressed extreme fear.

I ran to her in an ecstasy of joy; I kissed and embraced her again and again. I ran to the bell and rang it vehemently, to bring others to the spot who might at once relieve my father's anxiety.

"Dear Carmilla, what has become of you all this time? We have been in agonies of anxiety about you," I exclaimed. "Where have you been? How did you come back?"

"Last night has been a night of wonders," she said.

"For mercy's sake, explain all you can."

"It was past two last night," she said, "when I went to sleep as usual in my bed, with my doors locked, that of the dressing room, and that opening upon the gallery. My sleep was uninterrupted, and, so far as I know, dreamless; but I woke just now on the sofa in the dressing room there, and I found the door between the rooms open, and the other door forced. How could all this have happened without my being wakened? It must have been accompanied with a great deal of noise, and I am particularly easily wakened; and how could I have been carried out of my bed without my sleep having been interrupted, I whom the slightest stir startles?"

By this time, Madame, Mademoiselle, my father, and a number of the servants were in the room. Carmilla was, of course, overwhelmed with inquiries, congratulations, and welcomes. She had but one story to tell, and seemed the least able of all the party to suggest any way of accounting for what had happened.

My father took a turn up and down the room, thinking. I saw Carmilla's eye follow him for a moment with a sly, dark glance.

When my father had sent the servants away, Mademoiselle having gone in search of a little bottle of valerian and sal-volatile, and there being no one now in the room with Carmilla, except my father, Madame, and myself, he came to her thoughtfully, took her hand very kindly, led her to the sofa, and sat down beside her.

"Will you forgive me, my dear, if I risk a conjecture, and ask a question?"

"Who can have a better right?" she said. "Ask what you please, and I will tell you everything. But my story is simply one of bewilderment and darkness. I know absolutely nothing. Put any question you please. But you know, of course, the limitations mamma has placed me under."

"Perfectly, my dear child. I need not approach the topics on which she desires our silence. Now, the marvel of last night consists in your having been removed from your bed and your room, without being wakened, and this removal having occurred apparently while the windows were still secured, and the two doors locked upon the inside. I will tell you my theory and ask you a question."

Carmilla was leaning on her hand dejectedly; Madame and I were listening breathlessly.

"Now, my question is this. Have you ever been suspected of walking in your sleep?"

"Never, since I was very young indeed."

"But you did walk in your sleep when you were young?"

"Yes; I know I did. I have been told so often by my old nurse."

My father smiled and nodded.

"Well, what has happened is this. You got up in your sleep, unlocked the door, not leaving the key, as usual, in the lock, but taking it out and locking it on the outside; you again took the key out, and carried it away with you to some one of the five-and-twenty rooms on this floor, or perhaps upstairs or downstairs. There are so many rooms and closets, so much heavy furniture, and such accumulations of lumber, that it would require a week to search this old house thoroughly. Do you see, now, what I mean?"

"I do, but not all," she answered.

"And how, papa, do you account for her finding herself on the sofa in the dressing room, which we had searched so carefully?"

"She came there after you had searched it, still in her sleep, and at last awoke spontaneously, and was as much surprised to find herself where she was as any one else. I wish all mysteries were as easily and innocently explained as yours, Carmilla," he said, laughing. "And so we may congratulate ourselves on the certainty that the most natural explanation of the occurrence is one that involves no drugging, no tampering with locks, no burglars, or poisoners, or witches—nothing that need alarm Carmilla, or anyone else, for our safety."

Carmilla was looking charmingly. Nothing could be more beautiful than her tints. Her beauty was, I think, enhanced by that graceful languor that was peculiar to her. I think my father was silently contrasting her looks with mine, for he said:

"I wish my poor Laura was looking more like herself"; and he sighed.

So our alarms were happily ended, and Carmilla restored to her friends.

CHAPTER IX.

THE DOCTOR

As Carmilla would not hear of an attendant sleeping in her room, my father arranged that a servant should sleep outside her door, so that she would not attempt to make another such excursion without being arrested at her own door.

That night passed quietly; and next morning early, the doctor, whom my father had sent for without telling me a word about it, arrived to see me.

Madame accompanied me to the library; and there the grave little doctor, with white hair and spectacles, whom I mentioned before, was waiting to receive me.

I told him my story, and as I proceeded he grew graver and graver.

We were standing, he and I, in the recess of one of the windows, facing one another. When my statement was over, he leaned with his shoulders against the wall, and with his eyes fixed on me earnestly, with an interest in which was a dash of horror.

After a minute's reflection, he asked Madame if he could see my father.

He was sent for accordingly, and as he entered, smiling, he said:

"I dare say, doctor, you are going to tell me that I am an old fool for having brought you here; I hope I am."

But his smile faded into shadow as the doctor, with a very grave face, beckoned him to him.

He and the doctor talked for some time in the same recess where I had just conferred with the physician. It seemed an earnest and argumentative conversation. The room is very large, and I and Madame stood together, burning with curiosity, at the farther end. Not a word could we hear, however, for they spoke in a very low tone, and the deep recess of the window quite concealed the doctor from view, and very nearly my father, whose foot, arm, and shoulder only could we see; and the voices were, I suppose, all the less audible for the sort of closet which the thick wall and window formed.

After a time my father's face looked into the room; it was pale, thoughtful, and, I fancied, agitated.

"Laura, dear, come here for a moment. Madame, we shan't trouble you, the doctor says, at present."

Accordingly I approached, for the first time a little alarmed; for, although I felt very weak, I did not feel ill; and strength, one always fancies, is a thing that may be picked up when we please.

My father held out his hand to me, as I drew near, but he was looking at the doctor, and he said:

"It certainly *is* very odd; I don't understand it quite. Laura, come here, dear; now attend to Doctor Spielsberg, and recollect yourself."

"You mentioned a sensation like that of two needles piercing the skin, somewhere about your neck, on the night when you experienced your first horrible dream. Is there still any soreness?"

"None at all," I answered.

"Can you indicate with your finger about the point at which you think this occurred?"

"Very little below my throat—here," I answered.

I wore a morning dress, which covered the place I pointed to.

"Now you can satisfy yourself," said the doctor. "You won't mind your papa's lowering your dress a very little. It is necessary, to detect a symptom of the complaint under which you have been suffering."

I acquiesced. It was only an inch or two below the edge of my collar.

"God bless me!—so it is," exclaimed my father, growing pale.

"You see it now with your own eyes," said the doctor, with a gloomy triumph.

"What is it?" I exclaimed, beginning to be frightened.

"Nothing, my dear young lady, but a small blue spot, about the size of the tip of your little finger; and now," he continued, turning to papa, "the question is what is best to be done?"

"Is there any danger?" I urged, in great trepidation.

"I trust not, my dear," answered the doctor. "I don't see why you should not recover. I don't see why you should not begin *immediately* to get better. That is the point at which the sense of strangulation begins?"

"Yes," I answered.

"And—recollect as well as you can—the same point was a kind of centre of that thrill which you described just now, like the current of a cold stream running against you?"

"It may have been; I think it was."

"Ay, you see?" he added, turning to my father. "Shall I say a word to Madame?"

"Certainly," said my father.

He called Madame to him, and said:

"I find my young friend here far from well. It won't be of any great consequence, I hope; but it will be necessary that some steps be taken, which I will explain by-and-by; but in the meantime, Madame, you will be so good as not to let Miss Laura be alone for one moment. That is the only direction I need give for the present. It is indispensable."

"We may rely upon your kindness, Madame, I know," added my father.

Madame satisfied him eagerly.

"And you, dear Laura, I know you will observe the doctor's direction."

"I shall have to ask your opinion upon another patient, whose symptoms slightly resemble those of my daughter, that have just been detailed to you—very much milder in degree, but I believe quite of the same sort. She is a young lady—our guest; but as you say you will be passing this way again this evening, you can't do better than take your supper here, and you can then see her. She does not come down till the afternoon."

"I thank you," said the doctor. "I shall be with you, then, at about seven this evening."

And then they repeated their directions to me and to Madame, and with this parting charge my father left us, and walked out with the doctor; and I saw them pacing together up and down between the road and the moat, on the grassy platform in front of the castle, evidently absorbed in earnest conversation.

The doctor did not return. I saw him mount his horse there, take his leave, and ride away eastward through the forest. Nearly at the same time I saw the man arrive from Dranfield with the letters, and dismount and hand the bag to my father.

In the meantime, Madame and I were both busy, lost in conjecture as to the reasons of the singular and earnest direction which the doctor and my father had concurred in imposing. Madame, as she afterwards told me, was afraid the doctor apprehended a sudden seizure, and that, without prompt assistance, I might either lose my life in a fit, or at least be seriously hurt.

The interpretation did not strike me; and I fancied, perhaps luckily for my nerves, that the arrangement was prescribed simply to secure a companion, who would prevent my taking too much exercise, or eating unripe fruit, or doing any of the fifty foolish things to which young people are supposed to be prone.

About half an hour after my father came in—he had a letter in his hand—and said:

"This letter had been delayed; it is from General Spielsdorf. He might have been here yesterday, he may not come till tomorrow or he may be here today."

He put the open letter into my hand; but he did not look pleased, as he used when a guest, especially one so much loved as the General, was coming. On the contrary, he looked as if he wished him at the bottom of the Red Sea. There was plainly something on his mind which he did not choose to divulge.

"Papa, darling, will you tell me this?" said I, suddenly laying my hand on his arm, and looking, I am sure, imploringly in his face.

"Perhaps," he answered, smoothing my hair caressingly over my eyes.

"Does the doctor think me very ill?"

"No, dear; he thinks, if right steps are taken, you will be quite well again, at least, on the high road to a complete recovery, in a day or two," he answered, a little dryly. "I wish our good friend, the General, had chosen any other time; that is, I wish you had been perfectly well to receive him."

"But do tell me, papa," I insisted, "*what* does he think is the matter with me?"

"Nothing; you must not plague me with questions," he answered, with more irritation than I ever remember him to have displayed before; and seeing that I looked wounded, I suppose, he kissed me, and added, "You shall know all about it in a day or two; that is, all that I know. In the meantime, you are not to trouble your head about it."

He turned and left the room, but came back before I had done wondering and puzzling over the oddity of all this; it was merely to say that he was going to Karnstein, and had ordered the carriage to be ready at twelve, and that I and Madame should accompany him; he was going to see the priest who lived near those picturesque grounds, upon business, and as Carmilla had never seen them, she could follow, when she came down, with Mademoiselle, who would bring materials for what you call a picnic, which might be laid for us in the ruined castle.

At twelve o'clock, accordingly, I was ready, and not long after, my father, Madame and I set out upon our projected drive. Passing the drawbridge we turn to the right, and follow the road over the steep Gothic bridge, westward, to reach the deserted village and ruined castle of Karnstein.

No sylvan drive can be fancied prettier. The ground breaks into gentle hills and hollows, all clothed with beautiful wood, totally destitute of the comparative formality which artificial planting and early culture and pruning impart.

The irregularities of the ground often lead the road out of its course, and cause it to wind beautifully round the sides of broken hollows and the steeper sides of the hills, among varieties of ground almost inexhaustible.

Turning one of these points, we suddenly encountered our old friend, the General, riding towards us, attended by a mounted servant. His portmanteaus were following in a hired wagon, such as we term a cart.

The General dismounted as we pulled up, and, after the usual greetings, was easily persuaded to accept the vacant seat in the carriage and send his horse on with his servant to the schloss.

CHAPTER X

BEREAVED

I t was about ten months since we had last seen him: but that time had sufficed to make an alteration of years in his appearance. He had grown thinner; something of gloom and anxiety had taken the place of that cordial serenity which used to characterize his features. His dark blue eyes, always penetrating, now gleamed with a sterner light from under his shaggy grey eyebrows. It was not such a change as grief alone usually induces, and angrier passions seemed to have had their share in bringing it about.

We had not long resumed our drive, when the General began to talk, with his usual soldierly directness, of the bereavement, as he termed it, which he had sustained in the death of his beloved niece and ward; and he then broke out in a tone of intense bitterness and fury, inveighing against the "hellish arts" to which she had fallen a victim, and expressing, with more exasperation than piety, his wonder that Heaven should tolerate so monstrous an indulgence of the lusts and malignity of hell.

My father, who saw at once that something very extraordinary had befallen, asked him, if not too painful to him, to detail the circumstances which he thought justified the strong terms in which he expressed himself.

"I should tell you all with pleasure," said the General, "but you would not believe me."

"Why should I not?" he asked.

"Because," he answered testily, "you believe in nothing but what consists with your own prejudices and illusions. I remember when I was like you, but I have learned better."

"Try me," said my father; "I am not such a dogmatist as you suppose. Besides which, I very well know that you generally require proof for what you believe, and am, therefore, very strongly pre-disposed to respect your conclusions."

"You are right in supposing that I have not been led lightly into a belief in the marvelous—for what I have experienced *is* marvel-ous—and I have been forced by extraordinary evidence to credit that which ran counter, diametrically, to all my theories. I have been made the dupe of a preternatural conspiracy."

Notwithstanding his professions of confidence in the General's penetration, I saw my father, at this point, glance at the General, with, as I thought, a marked suspicion of his sanity.

The General did not see it, luckily. He was looking gloomily and curiously into the glades and vistas of the woods that were opening before us.

"You are going to the Ruins of Karnstein?" he said. "Yes, it is a lucky coincidence; do you know I was going to ask you to bring me there to inspect them. I have a special object in exploring. There is a ruined chapel, ain't there, with a great many tombs of that extinct family?"

"So there are—highly interesting," said my father. "I hope you are thinking of claiming the title and estates?"

My father said this gaily, but the General did not recollect the laugh, or even the smile, which courtesy exacts for a friend's joke; on the contrary, he looked grave and even fierce, ruminating on a matter that stirred his anger and horror.

"Something very different," he said, gruffly. "I mean to unearth some of those fine people. I hope, by God's blessing, to accomplish a pious sacrilege here, which will relieve our earth of certain monsters, and enable honest people to sleep in their beds without being assailed by murderers. I have strange things to tell you, my dear friend, such as I myself would have scouted as incredible a few months since."

My father looked at him again, but this time not with a glance of suspicion—with an eye, rather, of keen intelligence and alarm.

"The house of Karnstein," he said, "has been long extinct: a hundred years at least. My dear wife was maternally descended from the Karnsteins. But the name and title have long ceased to exist. The castle is a ruin; the very village is deserted; it is fifty years since the smoke of a chimney was seen there; not a roof left."

"Quite true. I have heard a great deal about that since I last saw you; a great deal that will astonish you. But I had better relate everything in the order in which it occurred," said the General. "You saw my dear ward—my child, I may call her. No creature could have been more beautiful, and only three months ago none more blooming."

"Yes, poor thing! when I saw her last she certainly was quite lovely," said my father. "I was grieved and shocked more than I can tell you, my dear friend; I knew what a blow it was to you."

He took the General's hand, and they exchanged a kind pressure. Tears gathered in the old soldier's eyes. He did not seek to conceal them. He said:

"We have been very old friends; I knew you would feel for me, childless as I am. She had become an object of very dear interest to me, and repaid my care by an affection that cheered my home and made my life happy. That is all gone. The years that remain to me on earth may not be very long; but by God's mercy I hope to accomplish a service to mankind before I die, and to subserve the vengeance of Heaven upon the fiends who have murdered my poor child in the spring of her hopes and beauty!"

"You said, just now, that you intended relating everything as it occurred," said my father. "Pray do; I assure you that it is not mere curiosity that prompts me."

By this time we had reached the point at which the Drunstall road, by which the General had come, diverges from the road which we were traveling to Karnstein.

"How far is it to the ruins?" inquired the General, looking anxiously forward.

"About half a league," answered my father. "Pray let us hear the story you were so good as to promise."

CHAPTER XI

THE STORY

With all my heart," said the General, with an effort; and after a short pause in which to arrange his subject, he commenced one of the strangest narratives I ever heard.

"My dear child was looking forward with great pleasure to the visit you had been so good as to arrange for her to your charming daughter." Here he made me a gallant but melancholy bow. "In the meantime we had an invitation to my old friend the Count Carlsfeld, whose schloss is about six leagues to the other side of Karnstein. It was to attend the series of fêtes which, you remember, were given by him in honor of his illustrious visitor, the Grand Duke Charles."

"Yes; and very splendid, I believe, they were," said my father.

"Princely! But then his hospitalities are quite regal. He has Aladdin's lamp. The night from which my sorrow dates was devoted to a magnificent masquerade. The grounds were thrown open, the trees hung with colored lamps. There was such a display of fireworks as Paris itself had never witnessed. And such music—music, you know, is my weakness—such ravishing music! The finest instrumental band, perhaps, in the world, and the finest singers who could be collected from all the great operas in Europe. As you wandered through these fantastically illuminated grounds, the moon-lighted château throwing a rosy light from its long rows of windows, you would suddenly hear these ravishing voices stealing from the silence of some grove, or rising from boats upon the lake. I felt myself, as I looked and listened, carried back into the romance and poetry of my early youth.

"When the fireworks were ended, and the ball beginning, we returned to the noble suite of rooms that were thrown open to the dancers. A masked ball, you know, is a beautiful sight; but so brilliant a spectacle of the kind I never saw before.

"It was a very aristocratic assembly. I was myself almost the only 'nobody' present.

"My dear child was looking quite beautiful. She wore no mask. Her excitement and delight added an unspeakable charm to her features, always lovely. I remarked a young lady, dressed magnificently, but wearing a mask, who appeared to me to be observing my ward with extraordinary interest. I had seen her, earlier in the evening, in the great hall, and again, for a few minutes, walking near us, on the terrace under the castle windows, similarly employed. A lady, also masked, richly and gravely dressed, and with a stately air, like a person of rank, accompanied her as a chaperon. Had the young lady not worn a mask, I could, of course, have been much more certain upon the question whether she was really watching my poor darling. I am now well assured that she was.

"We were now in one of the *salons*. My poor dear child had been dancing, and was resting a little in one of the chairs near the door; I was standing near. The two ladies I have mentioned had approached and the younger took the chair next my ward; while her companion stood beside me, and for a little time addressed herself, in a low tone, to her charge.

"Availing herself of the privilege of her mask, she turned to me, and in the tone of an old friend, and calling me by my name, opened a conversation with me, which piqued my curiosity a good deal. She referred to many scenes where she had met me—at Court, and at distinguished houses. She alluded to little incidents which I had long ceased to think of, but which, I found, had only lain in abeyance in my memory, for they instantly started into life at her touch.

"I became more and more curious to ascertain who she was, every moment. She parried my attempts to discover very adroitly and pleasantly. The knowledge she showed of many passages in my life seemed to me all but unaccountable; and she appeared to take a not unnatural pleasure in foiling my curiosity, and in seeing me flounder in my eager perplexity, from one conjecture to another.

"In the meantime the young lady, whom her mother called by the odd name of Millarca, when she once or twice addressed her, had, with the same ease and grace, got into conversation with my ward.

"She introduced herself by saying that her mother was a very old acquaintance of mine. She spoke of the agreeable audacity which a mask rendered practicable; she talked like a friend; she admired her dress, and insinuated very prettily her admiration of her beauty. She amused her with laughing criticisms upon the people who crowded the ballroom, and laughed at my poor child's fun. She was very witty and lively when she pleased, and after a time they had grown very good friends, and the young stranger lowered her mask, displaying a remarkably beautiful face. I had never seen it before, neither had my dear child. But though it was new to us, the features were so engaging, as well as lovely, that it was impossible not to feel the attraction powerfully. My poor girl did so. I never saw anyone more taken with another at first sight, unless, indeed, it was the stranger herself, who seemed quite to have lost her heart to her.

"In the meantime, availing myself of the license of a masquerade, I put not a few questions to the elder lady.

"'You have puzzled me utterly,' I said, laughing. 'Is that not enough? Won't you, now, consent to stand on equal terms, and do me the kindness to remove your mask?'

"'Can any request be more unreasonable?' she replied. 'Ask a lady to yield an advantage! Beside, how do you know you should recognize me? Years make changes.'

"'As you see,' I said, with a bow, and, I suppose, a rather melancholy little laugh.

"'As philosophers tell us,' she said; 'and how do you know that a sight of my face would help you?'

"'I should take chance for that,' I answered. 'It is vain trying to make yourself out an old woman; your figure betrays you.'

"'Years, nevertheless, have passed since I saw you, rather since you saw me, for that is what I am considering. Millarca, there, is my daughter; I cannot then be young, even in the opinion of people whom time has taught to be indulgent, and I may not like to be compared with what you remember me. You have no mask to remove. You can offer me nothing in exchange.'

"'My petition is to your pity, to remove it.'

"'And mine to yours, to let it stay where it is,' she replied.

"'Well, then, at least you will tell me whether you are French or German; you speak both languages so perfectly.'

"'I don't think I shall tell you that, General; you intend a surprise, and are meditating the particular point of attack.'

"'At all events, you won't deny this,' I said, 'that being honored by your permission to converse, I ought to know how to address you. Shall I say Madame la Comtesse?'

"She laughed, and she would, no doubt, have met me with another evasion—if, indeed, I can treat any occurrence in an interview every circumstance of which was prearranged, as I now believe, with the profoundest cunning, as liable to be modified by accident.

"'As to that,' she began; but she was interrupted, almost as she opened her lips, by a gentleman, dressed in black, who looked particularly elegant and distinguished, with this drawback, that his face was the most deadly pale I ever saw, except in death. He was in no masquerade—in the plain evening dress of a gentleman;

and he said, without a smile, but with a courtly and unusually
low bow:

"'Will Madame la Comtesse permit me to say a very few words
which may interest her?'

"The lady turned quickly to him, and touched her lip in token
of silence; she then said to me, 'Keep my place for me, General; I
shall return when I have said a few words.'

"And with this injunction, playfully given, she walked a little
aside with the gentleman in black, and talked for some minutes,
apparently very earnestly. They then walked away slowly together
in the crowd, and I lost them for some minutes.

"I spent the interval in cudgeling my brains for a conjecture as
to the identity of the lady who seemed to remember me so kindly,
and I was thinking of turning about and joining in the conversation
between my pretty ward and the Countess's daughter, and trying
whether, by the time she returned, I might not have a surprise in
store for her, by having her name, title, chateau, and estates at my
fingers' ends. But at this moment she returned, accompanied by
the pale man in black, who said:

"'I shall return and inform Madame la Comtesse when her
carriage is at the door.'

"He withdrew with a bow."

CHAPTER XII.

A PETITION

" 'Then we are to lose Madame la Comtesse, but I hope only for a few hours,' I said, with a low bow.

"'It may be that only, or it may be a few weeks. It was very unlucky his speaking to me just now as he did. Do you now know me?'

"I assured her I did not.

"'You shall know me,' she said, 'but not at present. We are older and better friends than, perhaps, you suspect. I cannot yet declare myself. I shall in three weeks pass your beautiful schloss, about which I have been making enquiries. I shall then look in upon you for an hour or two, and renew a friendship which I never think of without a thousand pleasant recollections. This moment a piece of news has reached me like a thunderbolt. I must set out now, and travel by a devious route, nearly a hundred miles, with all the dispatch I can possibly make. My perplexities multiply. I am only deterred by the compulsory reserve I practice as to my name from making a very singular request of you. My poor child has not quite recovered her strength. Her horse fell with her, at a hunt which she had ridden out to witness, her nerves have not yet recovered the shock, and our physician says that she must on no account exert herself for some time to come. We came here, in consequence, by very easy stages—hardly six leagues a day. I must now travel day and night, on a mission of life and death—a mission the critical and momentous nature of which I shall be able to explain to you when we meet, as I hope we shall, in a few weeks, without the necessity of any concealment.'

"She went on to make her petition, and it was in the tone of a person from whom such a request amounted to conferring, rather than seeking a favor. This was only in manner, and, as it seemed, quite unconsciously. Than the terms in which it was expressed, nothing could be more deprecatory. It was simply that I would consent to take charge of her daughter during her absence.

"This was, all things considered, a strange, not to say, an audacious request. She in some sort disarmed me, by stating and admitting everything that could be urged against it, and throwing herself entirely upon my chivalry. At the same moment, by a fatality that seems to have predetermined all that happened, my poor child came to my side, and, in an undertone, besought me to invite her new friend, Millarca, to pay us a visit. She had just been sounding her, and thought, if her mamma would allow her, she would like it extremely.

"At another time I should have told her to wait a little, until, at least, we knew who they were. But I had not a moment to think in. The two ladies assailed me together, and I must confess the refined and beautiful face of the young lady, about which there was something extremely engaging, as well as the elegance and fire of high birth, determined me; and, quite overpowered, I submitted, and undertook, too easily, the care of the young lady, whom her mother called Millarca.

"The Countess beckoned to her daughter, who listened with grave attention while she told her, in general terms, how suddenly and peremptorily she had been summoned, and also of the arrangement she had made for her under my care, adding that I was one of her earliest and most valued friends.

"I made, of course, such speeches as the case seemed to call for, and found myself, on reflection, in a position which I did not half like.

"The gentleman in black returned, and very ceremoniously conducted the lady from the room.

"The demeanor of this gentleman was such as to impress me with the conviction that the Countess was a lady of very much more importance than her modest title alone might have led me to assume.

"Her last charge to me was that no attempt was to be made to learn more about her than I might have already guessed, until her return. Our distinguished host, whose guest she was, knew her reasons.

"'But here,' she said, 'neither I nor my daughter could safely remain for more than a day. I removed my mask imprudently for a moment, about an hour ago, and, too late, I fancied you saw me. So I resolved to seek an opportunity of talking a little to you. Had I found that you *had* seen me, I would have thrown myself on your high sense of honor to keep my secret some weeks. As it is, I am satisfied that you did not see me; but if you now *suspect*, or, on reflection, *should* suspect, who I am, I commit myself, in like manner, entirely to your honor. My daughter will observe the same secrecy, and I well know that you will, from time to time, remind her, lest she should thoughtlessly disclose it.'

"She whispered a few words to her daughter, kissed her hurriedly twice, and went away, accompanied by the pale gentleman in black, and disappeared in the crowd.

"'In the next room,' said Millarca, 'there is a window that looks upon the hall door. I should like to see the last of mamma, and to kiss my hand to her.'

"We assented, of course, and accompanied her to the window. We looked out, and saw a handsome old-fashioned carriage, with a troop of couriers and footmen. We saw the slim figure of the pale gentleman in black, as he held a thick velvet cloak, and placed it about her shoulders and threw the hood over her head. She nodded to him, and just touched his hand with hers. He bowed low repeatedly as the door closed, and the carriage began to move.

"'She is gone,' said Millarca, with a sigh.

"'She is gone,' I repeated to myself, for the first time—in the hurried moments that had elapsed since my consent—reflecting upon the folly of my act.

"'She did not look up,' said the young lady, plaintively.

"'The Countess had taken off her mask, perhaps, and did not care to show her face,' I said; 'and she could not know that you were in the window.'

"She sighed and looked in my face. She was so beautiful that I relented. I was sorry I had for a moment repented of my hospitality, and I determined to make her amends for the unavowed churlishness of my reception.

"The young lady, replacing her mask, joined my ward in persuading me to return to the grounds, where the concert was soon to be renewed. We did so, and walked up and down the terrace that lies under the castle windows. Millarca became very intimate with us, and amused us with lively descriptions and stories of most of the great people whom we saw upon the terrace. I liked her more and more every minute. Her gossip, without being ill-natured, was extremely diverting to me, who had been so long out of the great world. I thought what life she would give to our sometimes lonely evenings at home.

"This ball was not over until the morning sun had almost reached the horizon. It pleased the Grand Duke to dance till then, so loyal people could not go away, or think of bed.

"We had just got through a crowded saloon, when my ward asked me what had become of Millarca. I thought she had been by her side, and she fancied she was by mine. The fact was, we had lost her.

"All my efforts to find her were vain. I feared that she had mistaken, in the confusion of a momentary separation from us, other people for her new friends, and had, possibly, pursued and lost them in the extensive grounds which were thrown open to us.

"Now, in its full force, I recognized a new folly in my having undertaken the charge of a young lady without so much as knowing her name; and fettered as I was by promises, of the reasons for imposing which I knew nothing, I could not even point my inquiries by saying that the missing young lady was the daughter of the Countess who had taken her departure a few hours before.

"Morning broke. It was clear daylight before I gave up my search. It was not till near two o'clock next day that we heard anything of my missing charge.

"At about that time a servant knocked at my niece's door, to say that he had been earnestly requested by a young lady, who appeared to be in great distress, to make out where she could find the General Baron Spielsdorf and the young lady his daughter, in whose charge she had been left by her mother.

"There could be no doubt, notwithstanding the slight inaccuracy, that our young friend had turned up; and so she had. Would to Heaven we had lost her!

"She told my poor child a story to account for her having failed to recover us for so long. Very late, she said, she had got to the housekeeper's bedroom in despair of finding us, and had then fallen into a deep sleep which, long as it was, had hardly sufficed to recruit her strength after the fatigues of the ball.

"That day Millarca came home with us. I was only too happy, after all, to have secured so charming a companion for my dear girl."

CHAPTER XIII.

THE WOODMAN

"There soon, however, appeared some drawbacks. In the first place, Millarca complained of extreme languor—the weakness that remained after her late illness—and she never emerged from her room till the afternoon was pretty far advanced. In the next place, it was accidentally discovered, although she always locked her door on the inside, and never disturbed the key from its place till she admitted the maid to assist at her toilet, that she was undoubtedly sometimes absent from her room in the very early morning, and at various times later in the day, before she wished it to be understood that she was stirring. She was repeatedly seen from the windows of the schloss, in the first faint grey of the morning, walking through the trees, in an easterly direction, and looking like a person in a trance. This convinced me that she walked in her sleep. But this hypothesis did not solve the puzzle.

How did she pass out from her room, leaving the door locked on the inside? How did she escape from the house without unbarring door or window?

"In the midst of my perplexities, an anxiety of a far more urgent kind presented itself.

"My dear child began to lose her looks and health, and that in a manner so mysterious, and even horrible, that I became thoroughly frightened.

"She was at first visited by appalling dreams; then, as she fancied, by a specter, sometimes resembling Millarca, sometimes in the shape of a beast, indistinctly seen, walking round the foot of her bed, from side to side. Lastly came sensations. One, not unpleasant, but very peculiar, she said, resembled the flow of an icy stream against her breast. At a later time, she felt something like a pair of large needles pierce her, a little below the throat, with a very sharp pain. A few nights after, followed a gradual and convulsive sense of strangulation; then came unconsciousness."

I could hear distinctly every word the kind old General was saying, because by this time we were driving upon the short grass that spreads on either side of the road as you approach the roofless village which had not shown the smoke of a chimney for more than half a century.

You may guess how strangely I felt as I heard my own symptoms so exactly described in those which had been experienced by the poor girl who, but for the catastrophe which followed, would have been at that moment a visitor at my father's château. You may suppose, also, how I felt as I heard him detail habits and mysterious peculiarities which were, in fact, those of our beautiful guest, Carmilla!

A vista opened in the forest; we were on a sudden under the chimneys and gables of the ruined village, and the towers and battlements of the dismantled castle, round which gigantic trees are grouped, overhung us from a slight eminence.

In a frightened dream I got down from the carriage, and in silence, for we had each abundant matter for thinking; we soon mounted the ascent, and were among the spacious chambers, winding stairs, and dark corridors of the castle.

"And this was once the palatial residence of the Karnsteins!" said the old General at length, as from a great window he looked out across the village, and saw the wide, undulating expanse of forest. "It was a bad family, and here its bloodstained annals were written," he continued. "It is hard that they should, after death, continue to plague the human race with their atrocious lusts. That is the chapel of the Karnsteins, down there."

He pointed down to the grey walls of the Gothic building partly visible through the foliage, a little way down the steep. "And I hear the axe of a woodman," he added, "busy among the trees that surround it; he possibly may give us the information of which I am in search, and point out the grave of Mircalla, Countess of Karnstein. These rustics preserve the local traditions of great families, whose stories die out among the rich and titled so soon as the families themselves become extinct."

"We have a portrait, at home, of Mircalla, the Countess Karnstein; should you like to see it?" asked my father.

"Time enough, dear friend," replied the General. "I believe that I have seen the original; and one motive which has led me to you earlier than I at first intended, was to explore the chapel which we are now approaching."

"What! see the Countess Mircalla," exclaimed my father; "why, she has been dead more than a century!"

"Not so dead as you fancy, I am told," answered the General.

"I confess, General, you puzzle me utterly," replied my father, looking at him, I fancied, for a moment with a return of the suspicion I detected before. But although there was anger and detestation, at times, in the old General's manner, there was nothing flighty.

"There remains to me," he said, as we passed under the heavy arch of the Gothic church—for its dimensions would have justified its being so styled—"but one object which can interest me during the few years that remain to me on earth, and that is to wreak on her the vengeance which, I thank God, may still be accomplished by a mortal arm."

"What vengeance can you mean?" asked my father, in increasing amazement.

"I mean, to decapitate the monster," he answered, with a fierce flush, and a stamp that echoed mournfully through the hollow ruin, and his clenched hand was at the same moment raised, as if it grasped the handle of an axe, while he shook it ferociously in the air.

"What?" exclaimed my father, more than ever bewildered.

"To strike her head off."

"Cut her head off!"

"Aye, with a hatchet, with a spade, or with anything that can cleave through her murderous throat. You shall hear," he answered, trembling with rage. And hurrying forward he said:

"That beam will answer for a seat; your dear child is fatigued; let her be seated, and I will, in a few sentences, close my dreadful story."

The squared block of wood, which lay on the grass-grown pavement of the chapel, formed a bench on which I was very glad to seat myself, and in the meantime the General called to the woodman, who had been removing some boughs which leaned upon the old walls; and, axe in hand, the hardy old fellow stood before us.

He could not tell us anything of these monuments; but there was an old man, he said, a ranger of this forest, at present sojourning in the house of the priest, about two miles away, who could point out every monument of the old Karnstein family; and, for a trifle, he undertook to bring him back with him, if we would lend him one of our horses, in little more than half an hour.

"Have you been long employed about this forest?" asked my father of the old man.

"I have been a woodman here," he answered in his *patois*, "under the forester, all my days; so has my father before me, and so on, as many generations as I can count up. I could show you the very house in the village here, in which my ancestors lived."

"How came the village to be deserted?" asked the General.

"It was troubled by *revenants*, sir; several were tracked to their graves, there detected by the usual tests, and extinguished in the usual way, by decapitation, by the stake, and by burning; but not until many of the villagers were killed.

"But after all these proceedings according to law," he continued—"so many graves opened, and so many vampires deprived of their horrible animation—the village was not relieved. But a Moravian nobleman, who happened to be traveling this way, heard how matters were, and being skilled—as many people are in his country—in such affairs, he offered to deliver the village from its tormentor. He did so thus: There being a bright moon that night, he ascended, shortly after sunset, the towers of the chapel here, from whence he could distinctly see the churchyard beneath him; you can see it from that window. From this point he watched until he saw the vampire come out of his grave, and place near it the linen clothes in which he had been folded, and then glide away towards the village to plague its inhabitants.

"The stranger, having seen all this, came down from the steeple, took the linen wrappings of the vampire, and carried them up to the top of the tower, which he again mounted. When the vampire returned from his prowlings and missed his clothes, he cried furiously to the Moravian, whom he saw at the summit of the tower, and who, in reply, beckoned him to ascend and take them. Whereupon the vampire, accepting his invitation, began to climb the steeple, and so soon as he had reached the battlements, the Moravian, with a stroke of his sword, clove his skull in twain, hurling him down to the churchyard, whither, descending by the winding stairs, the stranger followed and cut his head off, and next day delivered it and the body to the villagers, who duly impaled and burnt them.

"This Moravian nobleman had authority from the then head of the family to remove the tomb of Mircalla, Countess Karnstein, which he did effectually, so that in a little while its site was quite forgotten."

"Can you point out where it stood?" asked the General, eagerly.

The forester shook his head, and smiled.

"Not a soul living could tell you that now," he said; "besides, they say her body was removed; but no one is sure of that either."

Having thus spoken, as time pressed, he dropped his axe and departed, leaving us to hear the remainder of the General's strange story.

CHAPTER XIV

THE MEETING

||
My beloved child," he resumed, "was now growing rapidly worse.
The physician who attended her had failed to produce the
slightest impression on her disease, for such I then supposed it
to be. He saw my alarm, and suggested a consultation. I called in
an abler physician, from Gratz. Several days elapsed before he
arrived. He was a good and pious, as well as a learned man. Having seen my poor ward together, they withdrew to my library to
confer and discuss. I, from the adjoining room, where I awaited
their summons, heard these two gentlemen's voices raised in
something sharper than a strictly philosophical discussion. I
knocked at the door and entered. I found the old physician from
Gratz maintaining his theory. His rival was combating it with
undisguised ridicule, accompanied with bursts of laughter. This

unseemly manifestation subsided and the altercation ended on my entrance.

"'Sir,' said my first physician, 'my learned brother seems to think that you want a conjuror, and not a doctor.'

"'Pardon me,' said the old physician from Gratz, looking displeased, 'I shall state my own view of the case in my own way another time. I grieve, Monsieur le Général, that by my skill and science I can be of no use. Before I go I shall do myself the honor to suggest something to you.'

"He seemed thoughtful, and sat down at a table and began to write. Profoundly disappointed, I made my bow, and as I turned to go, the other doctor pointed over his shoulder to his companion who was writing, and then, with a shrug, significantly touched his forehead.

"This consultation, then, left me precisely where I was. I walked out into the grounds, all but distracted. The doctor from Gratz, in ten or fifteen minutes, overtook me. He apologized for having followed me, but said that he could not conscientiously take his leave without a few words more. He told me that he could not be mistaken; no natural disease exhibited the same symptoms; and that death was already very near. There remained, however, a day, or possibly two, of life. If the fatal seizure were at once arrested, with great care and skill her strength might possibly return. But all hung now upon the confines of the irrevocable. One more assault might extinguish the last spark of vitality which is, every moment, ready to die.

"'And what is the nature of the seizure you speak of?' I entreated.

"'I have stated all fully in this note, which I place in your hands upon the distinct condition that you send for the nearest clergyman, and open my letter in his presence, and on no account read it till he is with you; you would despise it else, and it is a matter of life and death. Should the priest fail you, then, indeed, you may read it.'

"He asked me, before taking his leave finally, whether I would wish to see a man curiously learned upon the very subject, which, after I had read his letter, would probably interest me above all others, and he urged me earnestly to invite him to visit him there; and so took his leave.

"The ecclesiastic was absent, and I read the letter by myself. At another time, or in another case, it might have excited my ridicule. But into what quackeries will not people rush for a last chance, where all accustomed means have failed, and the life of a beloved object is at stake?

"Nothing, you will say, could be more absurd than the learned man's letter. It was monstrous enough to have consigned him to a madhouse. He said that the patient was suffering from the visits of a vampire! The punctures which she described as having occurred near the throat, were, he insisted, the insertion of those two long, thin, and sharp teeth which, it is well known, are peculiar to vampires; and there could be no doubt, he added, as to the well-defined presence of the small livid mark which all concurred in describing as that induced by the demon's lips, and every symptom described by the sufferer was in exact conformity with those recorded in every case of a similar visitation.

"Being myself wholly skeptical as to the existence of any such portent as the vampire, the supernatural theory of the good doctor furnished, in my opinion, but another instance of learning and intelligence oddly associated with some one hallucination. I was so miserable, however, that, rather than try nothing, I acted upon the instructions of the letter.

"I concealed myself in the dark dressing room, that opened upon the poor patient's room, in which a candle was burning, and watched there till she was fast asleep. I stood at the door, peeping through the small crevice, my sword laid on the table beside me, as my directions prescribed, until, a little after one, I saw a large black object, very ill-defined, crawl, as it seemed to me, over the foot of the bed, and swiftly spread itself up to the poor girl's throat, where it swelled, in a moment, into a great, palpitating mass.

"For a few moments I had stood petrified. I now sprang forward, with my sword in my hand. The black creature suddenly contracted towards the foot of the bed, glided over it, and, standing on the floor about a yard below the foot of the bed, with a glare of skulking ferocity and horror fixed on me, I saw Millarca. Speculating I know not what, I struck at her instantly with my sword; but I saw her standing near the door, unscathed. Horrified, I pursued, and struck again. She was gone! and my sword flew to shivers against the door.

"I can't describe to you all that passed on that horrible night. The whole house was up and stirring. The specter Millarca was gone. But her victim was sinking fast, and before the morning dawned, she died."

The old General was agitated. We did not speak to him. My father walked to some little distance, and began reading the inscriptions on the tombstones; and thus occupied, he strolled into the door of a side chapel to prosecute his researches. The General leaned against the wall, dried his eyes, and sighed heavily. I was relieved on hearing the voices of Carmilla and Madame, who were at that moment approaching. The voices died away.

In this solitude, having just listened to so strange a story, connected, as it was, with the great and titled dead, whose monuments were moldering among the dust and ivy round us, and every incident of which bore so awfully upon my own mysterious case—in this haunted spot, darkened by the towering foliage that rose on every side, dense and high above its noiseless walls—a horror began to steal over me, and my heart sank as I thought that my friends were, after all, not about to enter and disturb this triste and ominous scene.

The old General's eyes were fixed on the ground, as he leaned with his hand upon the basement of a shattered monument.

Under a narrow, arched doorway, surmounted by one of those demoniacal grotesques in which the cynical and ghastly fancy of old Gothic carving delights, I saw very gladly the beautiful face and figure of Carmilla enter the shadowy chapel.

I was just about to rise and speak, and nodded smiling, in answer to her peculiarly engaging smile; when with a cry, the old man by my side caught up the woodman's hatchet, and started forward. On seeing him a brutalized change came over her features. It was an instantaneous and horrible transformation, as she made a crouching step backwards. Before I could utter a scream, he struck at her with all his force, but she dived under his blow, and unscathed, caught him in her tiny grasp by the wrist. He struggled for a moment to release his arm, but his hand opened, the axe fell to the ground, and the girl was gone.

He staggered against the wall. His grey hair stood upon his head, and a moisture shone over his face, as if he were at the point of death.

The frightful scene had passed in a moment. The first thing I recollect after, is Madame standing before me, and impatiently repeating again and again, the question, "Where is Mademoiselle Carmilla?"

I answered at length, "I don't know—I can't tell—she went there," and I pointed to the door through which Madame had just entered; "only a minute or two since."

"But I have been standing there, in the passage, ever since Mademoiselle Carmilla entered; and she did not return."

She then began to call "Carmilla" through every door and passage and from the windows, but no answer came.

"She called herself Carmilla?" asked the General, still agitated.

"Carmilla, yes," I answered.

"Aye," he said; "that is Millarca. That is the same person who long ago was called Mircalla, Countess Karnstein. Depart from this accursed ground, my poor child, as quickly as you can. Drive to the clergyman's house, and stay there till we come. Begone! May you never behold Carmilla more; you will not find her here."

CHAPTER XV.

ORDEAL AND EXECUTION

As he spoke, one of the strangest looking men I ever beheld entered the chapel at the door through which Carmilla had made her entrance and her exit. He was tall, narrow-chested, stooping, with high shoulders, and dressed in black. His face was brown and dried in with deep furrows; he wore an oddly-shaped hat with a broad leaf. His hair, long and grizzled, hung on his shoulders. He wore a pair of gold spectacles, and walked slowly, with an odd shambling gait, with his face sometimes turned up to the sky, and sometimes bowed down towards the ground, seemed to wear a perpetual smile; his long thin arms were swinging, and his lank hands, in old black gloves ever so much too wide for them, waving and gesticulating in utter abstraction.

"The very man!" exclaimed the General, advancing with manifest delight. "My dear Baron, how happy I am to see you, I had no hope of meeting you so soon." He signed to my father, who had by this time returned, and leading the fantastic old gentleman, whom he called the Baron to meet him. He introduced him formally, and they at once entered into earnest conversation. The stranger took a roll of paper from his pocket, and spread it on the worn surface of a tomb that stood by. He had a pencil case in his fingers, with which he traced imaginary lines from point to point on the paper, which from their often glancing from it, together, at certain points of the building, I concluded to be a plan of the chapel. He accompanied what I may term his lecture with occasional readings from a dirty little book, whose yellow leaves were closely written over.

They sauntered together down the side aisle, opposite to the spot where I was standing, conversing as they went; then they began measuring distances by paces, and finally they all stood together, facing a piece of the sidewall, which they began to examine with great minuteness; pulling off the ivy that clung over it, and rapping the plaster with the ends of their sticks, scraping here, and knocking there. At length they ascertained the existence of a broad marble tablet, with letters carved in relief upon it.

With the assistance of the woodman, who soon returned, a monumental inscription, and carved escutcheon, were disclosed. They proved to be those of the long lost monument of Mircalla, Countess Karnstein.

The old General, though not I fear given to the praying mood, raised his hands and eyes to heaven, in mute thanksgiving for some moments.

"Tomorrow," I heard him say; "the commissioner will be here, and the Inquisition will be held according to law."

Then turning to the old man with the gold spectacles, whom I have described, he shook him warmly by both hands and said:

"Baron, how can I thank you? How can we all thank you? You will have delivered this region from a plague that has scourged its inhabitants for more than a century. The horrible enemy, thank God, is at last tracked."

My father led the stranger aside, and the General followed. I knew that he had led them out of hearing, that he might relate my case, and I saw them glance often quickly at me, as the discussion proceeded.

My father came to me, kissed me again and again, and leading me from the chapel, said:

"It is time to return, but before we go home, we must add to our party the good priest, who lives but a little way from this; and persuade him to accompany us to the schloss."

In this quest we were successful: and I was glad, being unspeakably fatigued when we reached home. But my satisfaction was changed to dismay, on discovering that there were no tidings of Carmilla. Of the scene that had occurred in the ruined chapel, no explanation was offered to me, and it was clear that it was a secret which my father for the present determined to keep from me.

The sinister absence of Carmilla made the remembrance of the scene more horrible to me. The arrangements for the night were singular. Two servants, and Madame were to sit up in my room that night; and the ecclesiastic with my father kept watch in the adjoining dressing room.

The priest had performed certain solemn rites that night, the purport of which I did not understand any more than I comprehended the reason of this extraordinary precaution taken for my safety during sleep.

I saw all clearly a few days later.

The disappearance of Carmilla was followed by the discontinuance of my nightly sufferings.

You have heard, no doubt, of the appalling superstition that prevails in Upper and Lower Styria, in Moravia, Silesia, in Turkish Serbia, in Poland, even in Russia; the superstition, so we must call it, of the Vampire.

If human testimony, taken with every care and solemnity, judicially, before commissions innumerable, each consisting of many members, all chosen for integrity and intelligence, and constituting reports more voluminous perhaps than exist upon any one other class of cases, is worth anything, it is difficult to deny, or even to doubt the existence of such a phenomenon as the Vampire.

For my part I have heard no theory by which to explain what I myself have witnessed and experienced, other than that supplied by the ancient and well-attested belief of the country.

The next day the formal proceedings took place in the Chapel of Karnstein. The grave of the Countess Mircalla was opened; and the General and my father recognized each his perfidious and beautiful guest, in the face now disclosed to view. The features, though a hundred and fifty years had passed since her funeral, were tinted with the warmth of life. Her eyes were open; no cadaverous smell exhaled from the coffin. The two medical men, one officially present, the other on the part of the promoter of the inquiry, attested the marvelous fact that there was a faint but appreciable respiration, and a corresponding action of the heart. The limbs were perfectly flexible, the flesh elastic; and the leaden coffin floated with blood, in which to a depth of seven inches, the body lay immersed. Here then, were all the admitted signs and proofs of vampirism. The body, therefore, in accordance with the ancient practice, was raised, and a sharp stake driven through the heart of the vampire, who uttered a piercing shriek at the moment, in all respects such as might escape from a living person in the last agony. Then the head was struck off, and a torrent of blood flowed from the severed neck. The body and head was next placed on a pile of wood, and reduced to ashes, which were thrown upon the river and borne away, and that territory has never since been plagued by the visits of a vampire.

My father has a copy of the report of the Imperial Commission, with the signatures of all who were present at these proceedings, attached in verification of the statement. It is from this official paper that I have summarized my account of this last shocking scene.

CHAPTER XVI.

CONCLUSION

I write all this you suppose with composure. But far from it; I cannot think of it without agitation. Nothing but your earnest desire so repeatedly expressed, could have induced me to sit down to a task that has unstrung my nerves for months to come, and reinduced a shadow of the unspeakable horror which years after my deliverance continued to make my days and nights dreadful, and solitude insupportably terrific.

Let me add a word or two about that quaint Baron Vordenburg, to whose curious lore we were indebted for the discovery of the Countess Mircalla's grave.

He had taken up his abode in Gratz, where, living upon a mere pittance, which was all that remained to him of the once princely estates of his family, in Upper Styria, he devoted himself to the minute and laborious investigation of the marvelously authenticated tradition of Vampirism. He had at his fingers' ends all the great and little works upon the subject. "Magia Posthuma," "Phlegon de Mirabilibus," "Augustinus de cura pro Mortuis," "Philosophicae et Christianae Cogitationes de Vampiris," by John Christofer Herenberg; and a thousand others, among which I remember only a few of those which he lent to my father. He had a voluminous digest of all the judicial cases, from which he had extracted a system of principles that appear to govern—some always, and others occasionally only—the condition of the vampire. I may mention, in passing, that the deadly pallor attributed to that sort of *revenants*, is a mere melodramatic fiction. They present, in the grave, and when they show themselves in human society, the appearance of healthy life. When disclosed to light in their coffins, they exhibit all the symptoms that are enumerated as those which proved the vampire-life of the long-dead Countess Karnstein.

How they escape from their graves and return to them for certain hours every day, without displacing the clay or leaving any trace of disturbance in the state of the coffin or the cerements, has always been admitted to be utterly inexplicable. The amphibious existence of the vampire is sustained by daily renewed slumber in the grave. Its horrible lust for living blood supplies the vigor of its waking existence. The vampire is prone to be fascinated with an engrossing vehemence, resembling the passion of love, by particular persons. In pursuit of these it will exercise inexhaustible patience and stratagem, for access to a particular object may be obstructed in a hundred ways. It will never desist until it has satiated its passion, and drained the very life of its coveted victim. But it will, in these cases, husband and protract its murderous enjoyment with the refinement of an epicure, and heighten it by the gradual approaches of an artful courtship. In these cases it seems to yearn for something like sympathy and consent. In ordinary ones it goes direct to its object, overpowers with violence, and strangles and exhausts often at a single feast.

The vampire is, apparently, subject, in certain situations, to special conditions. In the particular instance of which I have given you a relation, Mircalla seemed to be limited to a name which, if not her real one, should at least reproduce, without the omission or addition of a single letter, those, as we say, anagrammatically, which compose it. *Carmilla* did this; so did *Millarca*.

My father related to the Baron Vordenburg, who remained with us for two or three weeks after the expulsion of Carmilla, the story about the Moravian nobleman and the vampire at Karnstein churchyard, and then he asked the Baron how he had discovered the exact position of the long-concealed tomb of the Countess Mircalla? The Baron's grotesque features puckered up into a mysterious smile; he looked down, still smiling on his worn spectacle case and fumbled with it. Then looking up, he said:

"I have many journals, and other papers, written by that remarkable man; the most curious among them is one treating of the visit of which you speak, to Karnstein. The tradition, of course, discolors and distorts a little. He might have been termed a Moravian nobleman, for he had changed his abode to that territory, and was, beside, a noble. But he was, in truth, a native of Upper

Styria. It is enough to say that in very early youth he had been a passionate and favored lover of the beautiful Mircalla, Countess Karnstein. Her early death plunged him into inconsolable grief. It is the nature of vampires to increase and multiply, but according to an ascertained and ghostly law.

"Assume, at starting, a territory perfectly free from that pest. How does it begin, and how does it multiply itself? I will tell you. A person, more or less wicked, puts an end to himself. A suicide, under certain circumstances, becomes a vampire. That specter visits living people in their slumbers; they die, and almost invariably, in the grave, develop into vampires. This happened in the case of the beautiful Mircalla, who was haunted by one of those demons. My ancestor, Vordenburg, whose title I still bear, soon discovered this, and in the course of the studies to which he devoted himself, learned a great deal more.

"Among other things, he concluded that suspicion of vampirism would probably fall, sooner or later, upon the dead Countess, who in life had been his idol. He conceived a horror, be she what she might, of her remains being profaned by the outrage of a posthumous execution. He has left a curious paper to prove that the vampire, on its expulsion from its amphibious existence, is projected into a far more horrible life; and he resolved to save his once beloved Mircalla from this.

"He adopted the stratagem of a journey here, a pretended removal of her remains, and a real obliteration of her monument. When age had stolen upon him, and from the vale of years, he looked back on the scenes he was leaving, he considered, in a different spirit, what he had done, and a horror took possession of him. He made the tracings and notes which have guided me to the very spot, and drew up a confession of the deception that he had practiced. If he had intended any further action in this matter, death prevented him; and the hand of a remote descendant has, too late for many, directed the pursuit to the lair of the beast."

We talked a little more, and among other things he said was this:

"One sign of the vampire is the power of the hand. The slender hand of Mircalla closed like a vice of steel on the General's wrist when he raised the hatchet to strike. But its power is not confined to its grasp; it leaves a numbness in the limb it seizes, which is slowly, if ever, recovered from."

The following Spring my father took me a tour through Italy. We remained away for more than a year. It was long before the terror of recent events subsided; and to this hour the image of Carmilla returns to memory with ambiguous alternations—sometimes the playful, languid, beautiful girl; sometimes the writhing fiend I saw in the ruined church; and often from a reverie I have started, fancying I heard the light step of Carmilla at the drawing room door.

The End

Jewelle Gomez, (Cabo Verdean/Wampanoag/Ioway; she/her), is a nov-elist, poet, essayist, playwright, and lesbian/feminist activist. Her work includes several poetry collections and the first Black Lesbian vampire novel, The Gilda Stories, in print for more than 30 years. She is a recipient of a Bram Stoker Legacy Award from Horror Writers of America.

Joseph Sheridan Le Fanu (1814-1873) was a popular and prolific Irish writer, specializing in gothic horror, mystery, ghost stories, and sensational fiction. The author of more than a dozen novels, he is widely recognized as an important pioneer in horror fiction.

OUR MISSION   Founded in 1982, Aunt Lute Books is an intersectional, feminist press dedicated to publishing literature by those who have been traditionally underrepresented in or excluded by the literary canon. Core to Aunt Lute's mission is the belief that the written word is critical to understanding and relating to each other as human beings. Through the centering of voices, perspectives, and stories that have not been traditionally welcomed by mainstream publishing, we strengthen ties across cultures and experiences, promoting a broader range of expression, and, we hope, working toward a more inclusive and just future.

LAND ACKNOWLEDGMENT   We, Aunt Lute Books, acknowledge that we do our work of uplifting marginalized voices and striving toward justice via the written word on the unceded ancestral homeland of the Ramaytush Ohlone who are the original inhabitants of the San Francisco Peninsula. As the indigenous stewards of this land and in accordance with their traditions, the Ramaytush Ohlone have never ceded, lost, nor forgotten their responsibilities as the caretakers of this place, as well as for all peoples who reside in their traditional territory. As Guests, we recognize that we benefit from living and working on their traditional homeland. We wish to pay our respects by acknowledging the Ancestors, Elders and Relatives of the Ramaytush Community and by affirming their sovereign rights as First Peoples.

You may buy books from our website.

www.auntlute.com

aunt lute books
P.O. Box 410687
San Francisco, CA 94141
books@auntlute.com

This book would not have been possible without the kind
contributions of the Aunt Lute Founding Friends:

Anonymous Donor	Diana Harris
Anonymous Donor	Phoebe Robins Hunter
Rusty Barceló	Diane Mosbacher, M.D., Ph.D.
Marian Bremer	Sara Paretsky
Marta Drury	William Preston, Jr.
Diane Goldstein	Elise Rymer Turner